CW01064616

MURDER AT MAPLEWOOD MANSION

A PARANORMAL COZY MYSTERY

HAUNTED HISTORIES
BOOK ONE

LYNN M. STOUT

CHAPTER 1

"Someone should write a book about your life," Ollie said.

"Pretty boring book," I grumbled as I poured myself another cup of coffee.

"Naw, it would be a mystery. But one with a happy ending. Like a cozy mystery. You know, bad stuff happens but then they find out whodunnit and everything works out in the end."

"Well, if that's the case, someone forgot the happy ending. As of now, things don't seem to be working out very well," I reminded my best friend.

"Be patient. The call will come." With those words of wisdom, she disconnected our call.

I laughed to myself. I am most definitely not a cozy mystery main character. I'm not young and plucky. I haven't recently inherited a deceased aunt's bakery, or craft shop, or knitting store, or bed-and-breakfast. I'm not returning home to start a new life or begin a fresh chapter.

I'm also not recently divorced or broken up with a longtime partner. I'm not in my seventies, running around town, sticking my nose into everyone's business with a gin and tonic in hand.

In fact, I'm quite boring. I've never been married and I love my career.

I have stable, loving people in my life. Of course, there's Ollie, my best friend since high school. And Gabby, my African Grey parrot.

I scratched my head, trying to think of the rest of my quirky crew. There! Yet another reason my life isn't a cozy mystery.

Honestly, there have been times when it's more like a horror novel.

My sister disappeared almost forty years ago when we were teenagers. I was the one who found her body hidden in the woods. So, yeah, definitely a horror novel.

And as of now, there was no happy ending in sight. The paranormal documentary I pitched to the network was still on hold and the call I'd been waiting for was not happening.

That's why Ollie had called. She was going to be my sound technician. My very first hire. But instead of good news. I had to tell her that there was still no news.

I sighed.

"It will be okay," Gabby squawked.

"Thanks, Gab," I said, stroking the bird's back.

Just as I got up, the phone rang.

It was official. My project got a green light, and I was the director of *Haunted Mysteries*, a paranormal documentary show. I'd spent the last several days assembling my team, and only had one position left to fill.

I stood on the sound stage watching an incredibly handsome man who was destined to make our viewers swoon. He was dressed immaculately, with teeth so white they glowed. His bright blue eyes were highlighted by perfect dark hair. His melodic voice was calm and soothing.

I sighed. Tyler Reed's on-camera presence was undeniable. He was suave, articulate, and handsome. He possessed the charm that would easily engage the attention of our mostly female viewership. The only problem was when the camera stopped rolling.

"He's a beautiful moving hazard," Ollie said.

"This has to be perfect, Ollie," I whispered. "This team has to be perfect."

When the camera stopped rolling, we watched in horror as Tyler tripped twice, simply walking off the set. His foot snagged on a cable, then he caught himself before falling, only to stumble towards Emily, our production assistant. In her sprightly youth she easily dodged out of his way at the last moment.

I sighed again.

"You need him, Jackie." The voice of Mia Sanchez was low and intolerant in my ear. She'd crept up behind us without a sound. This had become the least of her annoying habits.

Mia was the producer of our show and was a blessing and a curse. We were both in our fifties and of the mind that women should help other women, especially in this male-dominated business. At least, I thought that was the case. Ever since she found out the show was paranormal, though, she had been argumentative and hostile. I wasn't sure anymore how to take her.

"I know," I said.

And I did know. Tyler was amazing when the camera rolled and that's what mattered. Plus, he was beautiful, and that was something to remember. We had to make sure everything was perfect. I took in the rest of the crew as they wrapped up the take. Leo Kim, the award-winning cinematographer, was squinting into the small screen of his camera, reviewing what he'd just recorded. Emily Nichols appeared to be searching for something. She was rifling through bags and jackets, while

Ethan Brooks, our researcher and historian, stood helplessly nearby. What was going on?

As usual, Ollie read my mind and voiced my thoughts. "What in the world is she looking for? And is Ethan stroking out on us?" She said, only partly joking.

"She should check the pocket of that jacket," I muttered.

"What?" Mia asked. "Check it for what? And can we please do something about her makeup?"

I bristled at the comment. Mia was talking about Emily, who was now proudly waving a pair of glasses in the air while Ethan cheered and clapped his hands. She had found them in Ethan's jacket and now that he could see, the two of them were huddled over a stack of papers, flipping through them animatedly. If I didn't know better, I would swear I was watching a doting old grandfather teaching his granddaughter the ropes of research.

The renowned author and historian had at least ten best sellers in the areas of paranormal investigation and the psychology of criminal minds. He also had an almost encyclopedic knowledge of hauntings and paranormal activity spanning the previous two centuries. He'd just retired from teaching at the local college when I approached him with my offer.

"Work with me for two years. Help me get this

show off the ground. We don't need to solve the cases, we just need to tell the stories. Report on the activity, debunk it if we can, otherwise, let the viewers decide for themselves. I'm not here to convince anyone of anything. I'm here to tell a story."

"I appreciate that, but I'm just not interested," Ethan had said as he showed me the door.

I gave him my card and asked him to call should he reconsider. After glancing down at it, he hesitated, then his expression changed.

"Jackie Thompson?" He'd asked. "As in Sophie Thompson's sister? I'm right, aren't I? I knew you looked familiar."

I had no choice. I didn't want to base my name, my reputation and career, on what had happened to my sister in 1986, but sometimes, it seemed, I wasn't the only one motivated by her death. When Ethan found out who I was, he agreed to help me. But only if I hired someone very special to him. He said he had a student who was bright, but young. Energetic, but inexperienced. He wanted to mentor her.

I'll admit it was shocking to meet the young Emily Nichols. She wore all black. Her hair was dyed black and her nails painted black as well. And her makeup was ... heavy. Back in my day we would have said she was 'goth,' but apparently that wasn't as frequent a term now. Instead, it was simply a fashion choice. Emily was sweet, smart, and witty. And Mia would do well not to underestimate her.

Thus, I had a very well-paid researcher on staff and a production assistant who was currently earning her paycheck by hunting for a pair of glasses. Well, paycheck earned...she found them, after all.

"It's time," Mia said. "Go earn your salary and get this show on the road."

The van rattled as we pulled up the long winding drive towards Maplewood Mansion. The towering, shadowy silhouette of the house against the evening sky made me shiver as I thought of all the movies I'd seen with a similar beginning. The innocent group arriving at the dark and foreboding house without a care in the world, only to be...

I told myself to knock it off. I put on what I hoped was a determined and confident smile. After all, this was our big break. We had the chance to uncover the secrets of this notorious haunted mansion, solve an unsolved murder, and hopefully prove our show's worth.

When the van stopped, I hopped out and stretched. "Alright, team, let's get to work," I said.

Tyler climbed out after me and immediately stumbled over his own feet, nearly dropping his notebook.

"Smooth Tyler," Ollie teased. "Try not to break a leg before we even start filming," she said, shooting me a look.

Tyler grinned sheepishly, adjusting his tie. "Just keeping everyone on their toes."

Leo, our cinematographer, hustled past us and had his camera running. He panned over the building and then got footage of the crew standing in front of the van. "This place is like something out of a Gothic novel," he murmured, more to himself than anyone else.

Ollie threw her sound gear over her shoulder and followed Leo into the mansion. "I'll start setting up the sound sensors in the library," she said. "That's where Evelyn Carter's body was found, right?"

I nodded. "Yeah, let's start there. Emily, will you and Ethan help Ollie and Leo with the setup?"

Emily bounced on her toes. "On it! Come on, Ethan, let's get going."

Ethan's eyes met mine, and he ran a hand over his grey and slightly balding head. "Wish I had just ten percent of that energy," he grumbled as he followed her at a more measured pace. Still, it took only a minute before his nose was buried in an old map of the mansion.

"Hey Emily," he raised his voice. "There are rumors of hidden passages all over this place," he said, his voice tinged with excitement. "We need to keep an eye out for any architectural anomalies."

"Got it!" Emily shouted back.

As the crew made its way inside, I felt a familiar weight settle on my shoulder. Gabby couldn't fly very far, but she flew well enough to move from her perch to my shoulder and, in short bursts, around a room. I think she liked the independence of choosing when to join me and when to hang back.

Mostly, she stuck to my side, and that was fine by me. She was a source of both comfort and comic relief between her sharp eyes and her even sharper tongue.

"Gabby, keep an eye out for any ghosts, will you?" I said.

She bobbed her head and squawked, "I see dead people! I see dead people!"

The air in the library was noticeably colder than in the rest of the house. Dust motes danced in the beams of sunlight coming through the dusty drapes, and the faint smell of old books and decay filled the room. We spread out, each of us taking our positions.

"Brrr, it's freezing in here," Ollie said, wrapping her arms around herself. "This place sure knows how to welcome us. Where's my sweatshirt," she muttered.

"There should be a thermostat, right?" Tyler said as he stumbled over an old, tattered rug.

"Yeah, there should be. This was a functioning bed-and-breakfast not too long ago." We all looked around in the usual places for some way to control the temperature, but to no avail. It would be sweater weather inside the old mansion.

"Okay, everyone, grab a jacket. It's going to be chilly. Ollie, let's set up the main sound sensor near the fireplace," I instructed. "Leo, can you get a wide shot of the room? We want to capture every angle. And Tyler, let's get some introductory footage as soon as you're ready."

"Got it," Leo replied as everyone else nodded.

Emily and Ethan were busy placing smaller sensors around the room, their movements precise and efficient. As they worked, Gabby mimicked their actions, her head bobbing up and down.

"It's showtime!" She chirped, earning a laugh from Emily.

"Beetlejuice, right?" She asked.

Gabby bobbed her head up and down.

I watched as Tyler fumbled with his microphone, nearly dropping it twice before he managed to clip it on his shirt.

"Tyler, can I help you?" I asked, trying to keep a straight face.

"Nah, I'm good. Just a little technical difficulty," he muttered, his cheeks flushing.

"Remember, we're here to make a serious documentary," I said, winking at him. "Try not to turn it into a blooper reel."

Tyler rolled his eyes but couldn't hide his grin. "I'll do my best, boss."

As the team finished setting up, I took a moment to soak in the atmosphere. This was it. We were finally beginning our investigation into the mysteries of Maplewood Mansion. The room seemed to pulse with a life of its own, the weight of its history pressing down on us.

"Alright, team," I said, clapping my hands together. "Let's get this show on the road. Ollie, are we ready to record?"

"All set," Ollie replied, her fingers dancing over the controls. "Let's see if we can catch any of those ghostly whispers."

Tyler took his position in front of the camera, his earlier clumsiness replaced by his on-camera persona. "I'm Tyler Reed, and welcome to 'Haunted Mysteries.' Tonight, we bring you to Maplewood Mansion, a place shrouded in legend and enigma. Join us as we delve into its haunted history and seek to uncover the truth behind the supernatural occurrences that have plagued this estate for decades."

As Tyler continued his introduction, I couldn't

help but feel a surge of pride. Despite the challenges and the skeptics, we were here, doing what we loved.

Gabby, sensing my determination, let out a soft, encouraging whistle. "The truth is out there," she said.

"Yes, it is Gabby," I murmured, giving her a gentle pat. "Yes, it is."

CHAPTER 2

The team quickly fell into a rhythm, each member absorbed in their tasks. As I supervised the setup, my mind wandered to the phone call that had brought us here. Philip Harper, the mansion's current owner, wanted to reopen it as a bed-and-breakfast. Unfortunately, the unsolved murder of Evelyn Carter was making it difficult. Word had gotten out that she had been murdered in the library in a gruesome fashion, bludgeoned with a fire poker, and now the mansion was haunted by her ghost. It wasn't the kind of haunting that made ghost hunters flock to a place, either. It was the kind that made people run scared. Philip wanted us to debunk the haunting once and for all.

"Either that, or get rid of her," he'd muttered.

My heart broke to hear him speak about the

spirit of an innocent victim that way. I shook my head to clear my mind of his chilling words.

"Hey! Ollie, how's it going?" I refocused. She was hunched over her soundboard, oversized, retro headphones firmly in place.

Ollie frowned. "We're picking up some weird interference. It's like... I don't know, static mixed with whispers."

"Already?" I asked as I walked over and began peering at the dials and monitors. Sure enough, the readings were all over the place. "Could it be the wiring?" I asked, though I knew Ollie would have already considered that.

"Checked it twice. Everything's connected properly," she replied, biting her lip. "It's almost like something, or someone, doesn't want us here," she said in an eerie singsong voice wiggling her fingers in the air.

"Ha ha. Just keep working on it, okay? We can't afford to miss anything because of technical glitches."

Ollie nodded, her fingers dancing over the controls. "I'll take care of it."

"Emily, where are the EMF meters?" I asked.

Of course, she immediately produced them and within minutes were were methodically moving through the library, scanning each corner with the meters. The devices emitted low beeps, showing normal levels of electromagnetic fields.

But as we approached the large ornate desk near the corner of the room, the beeping grew more rapid.

"Looks like we found something," I said, feeling a mixture of excitement and trepidation. I knelt down, examining the desk more closely. It was an impressive piece of furniture, it's dark wood polished to a deep sheen.

"Where's this coming from?" Emily asked.

"Maybe behind it? Or behind the wall?" I suggested.

We worked to shove the desk away from the wall and ultimately revealed a small inconspicuous panel. My heart raced as I pried it open. Inside was a tangled mess of old wiring and a small dusty radio.

"Well, that explains the interference," I muttered, pulling the radio out and examining it. "This thing must be decades old."

Emily leaned over my shoulder, her eyes wide with curiosity. "Do you think it's still functional?"

"Hard to say," I replied, turning it over in my hands. "But it might be worth checking out. Ollie will get it working."

Just as I set the radio next to Ollie, Leo called out from across the room. "Jackie, I think I've got something!"

I hurried over to his station, where he was staring intently at the monitor.

"Look at this," he said, pointing to the screen. It showed a grainy image of the library, but there was something strange. In the frame's corner, near the spot where Evelyn's body had been found, a faint ghostly figure was visible. It flickered in and out of view, almost as if it were trying to manifest fully.

I looked at the spot in the room where the figure should have been and saw nothing. Then back at the monitor where the faint figure could still be seen, fading in and out. Then back at the still empty spot in the room. Then I looked at Leo.

"Yeah, I know," he said. "What do you think it means?"

All that went through my head was Gabby's quote from earlier, "I see dead people."

"I don't know," I finally said. "But whatever it is, it's definitely not a trick of the light."

I turned to the rest of the team. "Everyone stay sharp. We're definitely seeing some unusual things. This place is for real."

Ethan, who had been quietly observing, nodded in agreement. "We'll sort this out, Jackie. One way or another."

I appreciated his confidence, but I couldn't shake the feeling that we were only scratching the surface of something much darker.

As the team settled into their tasks and the initial hustle and bustle of setting up equipment quieted down, I found a moment to step outside. The mansion's grand architecture loomed above me, its shadow stretching out like a dark omen against the dimming sky. I leaned against one of the stone pillars on the porch, allowing myself a rare moment of introspection.

This was the moment I had been working toward for years. After countless hours of laboring behind the scenes on various production sets, I was finally directing my show. It felt surreal, like a dream teetering on the edge of reality.

My journey with the production company had been long and winding. I started as a lowly production assistant, running coffee and making endless copies. It wasn't glamorous, but it was a foot in the door. The paranormal and true crime had always fascinated me ever since I was a little girl. My grandmother and I would sit for hours watching documentaries about unsolved mysteries and haunted houses. Her influence had been profound, shaping my interests and career aspirations.

It was during those formative years that I first met Ollie. High school had been a mixed bag of experiences, but finding a kindred spirit in Ollie was like discovering a hidden treasure. We bonded over our love of all things spooky and unexplained, our friendship growing stronger with each passing year. Of course, Ollie was my first hire. It was an easy decision. Her tech skills were unparalleled, and her unwavering support made her an invaluable part of the team.

As if on cue, Gabby rubbed her head against mine. I think she sensed my sadness at times like this. Before becoming mine, the African Grey parrot had been my grandmother's. After she passed away, inheriting Gabby had been like inheriting a piece of my grandmother herself. They used to watch those same documentaries together, and Gabby had picked up an uncanny number of phrases from those days.

"It will be okay," Gabby said, repeating a saying my grandmother used often.

I couldn't help but smile. "I know, Gabby," I said, stroking her feathers.

My grandmother had been my biggest supporter, always encouraging my curiosity and passion for the unexplained. Losing her had been one of the hardest moments of my life. And I suspected Gabby missed her too.

A soft beep from my earpiece pulled me from my reverie. Ollie's voice crackled through, filled with the kind of urgency that told me something was up. "Jackie, we've got some strong readings in the basement. We're going to check it out. Want to come?"

"On my way," I replied.

As I headed inside, my mind refocused on the task at hand. Ollie was still hunched over her soundboard, her large headphones firmly in place. Emily and Ethan were still poring over a stack of old documents, their heads bent together in concentration.

Ollie glanced up and saw me. "Ready?" She asked.

"Yup, let's see what the basement has in store for us."

Everyone wanted to explore, so as a group, we descended the creaky stairs into the dark, chilly depths of the basement. I felt a mix of anticipation and nervous energy.

The basement air was thick with dust and the unmistakable scent of mildew. The overhead lights had burned out, so we turned on our flashlights, which cut through the gloom immediately. The basement was a sprawling space cluttered with old furniture, dusty crates, and cobwebs. Every step we took echoed off the stone walls.

"Ugh," Ethan said. "My flashlight battery is dead."

"Just use your phone," Emily suggested. "I'll change those batteries when we go back up."

Ethan hesitated then pulled his phone from a pocket. He looked at it, turned it over, then looked up helplessly at Emily.

She laughed. "Here. Use my flashlight and I'll use my phone. Remind me to show you how to do this. You never know when you might need your phone's light."

"Thank," he said as he took the flashlight.

"Hey everyone. Look at this," Tyler called out. He'd immediately been drawn to a large, musty chest.

We gathered around, our breath visible in the basement's chill while Ollie bent over next to Tyler.

"This thing looks ancient," she said, inspecting the lock.

"Can you open it?" I asked.

Tyler easily pried the lock open. With a satisfied grin, he lifted the heavy lid which immediately came away from the hinges and crashed to the floor. Everyone jumped back.

"Oops, sorry," Tyler said. "It's open now," he added sheepishly.

As our heart rates returned to normal, we all peeked inside. It appeared to be stacks of old letters and photographs, all yellowed with age and damp with time.

"Jackpot," Ethan whispered, carefully lifting

one letter. "We'll need to go through these," he said, his eyes shining.

Emily leaned in for a better look. "This is amazing," she said, her dark eyes wide. "I can help you, right?"

Ethan nodded. "Absolutely. Let's get these back upstairs, where we can examine them properly."

Ethan carefully handed each of us a bundle and we trudged back up the stairs.

"Papers wouldn't explain the readings we had, though," Leo said. "Should we go back down?"

I was about to let him know we had plenty of time to go back down later when a loud bang echoed through the hallway.

The source of the noise was soon apparent as Bob Lawson, the Harper family's attorney, burst through the door and stormed up to me.

"Miss Thompson," he greeted me curtly. "I remind you that this mansion is a functioning bed-and-breakfast. Any damage you cause will be charged to your production company." He looked at the bundles of paper and photos I was still holding.

I met his gaze steadily, not wanting to show any sign of intimidation. "And hello to you," I said. "We aren't doing any damage. We just got here. And from what I understand, this isn't a functioning bed-and-breakfast. That's why we're here in the first place."

Lawson's eyes narrowed. "No one wants you here snooping around, but the family needs the income from the hotel. You either need to prove this place isn't haunted or prove that any spirits here aren't malevolent. Then maybe we can get some guests again. Or at least paying ghost hunters."

What was this guy's problem? "We understand your concerns," I said, trying to keep my tone calm and professional. "But I would also like to find out who killed Evelyn, since the police seem to have given up on that front."

My timing couldn't have been better. Detective Ryan entered the mansion just as I said that and, of course, bristled at my remark. "We're doing everything we can with the resources we have, Miss Thompson."

"With all due respect, Detective, it's been decades," I replied, holding his gaze. "Maybe it's time for a fresh perspective."

Lawson cleared his throat, cutting through the tension. "Just remember, any damage or disturbance will not be tolerated. We need this investigation to be discreet and efficient."

"Of course," I assured him. "We'll handle everything with the utmost care. Like we always do."

Without missing a beat, Gabby echoed my last few words. "We always do," she squawked.

Lawson did a double-take and nodded towards

Gabby. "I hope that thing isn't tearing up the house."

I felt Gabby's feathers bristle and put a hand on her back.

Before I could say anything in her defense, Lawson said, "Now, if you'll excuse me, I have other matters to attend to. Come along, Ryan," he added, pivoting on one foot. Ryan shot me a look and followed Lawson outside, allowing the door to slam closed behind him.

"Well, that was fun," I said.

"That guy's a real peach," Ollie added.

The team nodded and mumbled their agreement as the tension slowly dissipated and they all moved back to the task at hand. Emily and Ethan were deep into the stacks of letters while Ollie and Leo were checking their equipment yet again.

I gave my stack of letters to Emily and then fiddled with the radio we'd found. I still felt drawn to it for some reason. It made me think about the other times I'd felt drawn towards something. I'd always had a knack for finding things. People, pets, sunglasses...I didn't fully understand it, but it had led me here and I was grateful.

CHAPTER 3

Tyler Reed: Take 1

The camera opens with a sweeping aerial shot of Maplewood Mansion, its Victorian architecture stark against the twilight sky. As the shot transitions to the front entrance, Tyler Reed steps into view, his demeanor confident and polished. He adjusts his tie, flashes a reassuring smile, and begins.

"Good evening. I'm Tyler Reed, and welcome to another spine-tingling episode of 'Haunted Histories,' where we delve into the darkest corners of the past to uncover the secrets of the supernatural. Tonight, we bring you a chilling tale from Maplewood Mansion, a place steeped in legend and enigma, where the echoes of the past refuse to be silenced."

The camera cuts to a wide shot of the mansion's grand facade, slowly zooming in on the intricately designed entrance.

"Nestled in the heart of a sleepy New England town, Maplewood Mansion stands as a testament to a bygone era. Built in the late 1800s by the enigmatic Harper family, this Victorian masterpiece has long been the subject of local lore and ghostly encounters. But what really lies behind its ornate doors and shadowy halls?"

The scene transitions to the mansion's dimly lit interior, where dust particles float in the air, caught in the beams of the setting sun.

"Our journey tonight centers on the tragic tale of Evelyn Carter, the town's beloved librarian. Evelyn was more than just a keeper of books—she was a seeker of truth, dedicated to uncovering the secrets of Maplewood Mansion before it became the charming bed-and-breakfast we see today."

The camera pans across old photographs of Evelyn, showing her in various settings: at the library, with a stack of old books, and standing in front of the mansion.

"Known for her relentless curiosity, Evelyn was researching the mansion's storied past, driven by rumors of its haunted history. But her quest for knowledge took a dark turn when she was found dead in the mansion's library. The police believe her murderer was a drifter, someone passing through town, but despite their efforts, the case remains unsolved."

Cut to a close-up of Tyler, his expression serious and contemplative.

"Since Evelyn's untimely death, the hauntings at Maplewood Mansion have intensified. Unexplained noises, ghostly apparitions, and chilling whispers have left the town's residents in fear. Many believe that Evelyn's spirit, along with other restless souls, still roams these halls, seeking justice and peace."

The camera shifts to Jackie and her team setting up equipment in the library, their faces illuminated by the glow of their monitors.

"To help us uncover the truth, we have the expertise of Jackie Thompson and her dedicated team of paranormal researchers. With state-of-the-art technology and a passion for solving mysteries, they are determined to delve into the mansion's dark history and bring light to its shadows."

The scene transitions to the basement, where the team discovers a musty old chest filled with letters and photographs.

"Despite the pressures and the haunting atmosphere, the team remains resolute. Not only driven by the desire to solve the mystery of Evelyn's death, but also to bring peace to the restless spirits that inhabit these walls."

"Our investigation is far from over. With each

passing moment, we get closer to unraveling the secrets of Maplewood Mansion. Will we finally uncover the truth behind Evelyn Carter's tragic fate? Or will the mysteries of this haunted house remain forever hidden?"

CHAPTER 4

As my thoughts drifted, I felt the weight of the investigation settle on my shoulders. As often happened during times of stress, memories from years ago resurfaced.

Soon my mind was drifting back to high school. Back to a time that should have been filled with the typical worries of teenage life like homework, crushes, and navigating friendships. Instead, it was a nightmare I could never wake up from.

My younger sister, Sophie, had disappeared without a trace. The panic that gripped our family was indescribable. I remembered the police coming to our house, the endless questions, the search parties combing through the neighborhood and surrounding areas. Despite all the efforts, there was no sign of her anywhere. It was as if she had vanished into thin air one day after school.

The nights that followed I had terrible night-mares. In my dreams, I saw a place deep in the woods, a clearing surrounded by tall, ancient trees. The image was so vivid that it felt more like a memory than a dream. I could see the exact spot, a patch of disturbed earth, the trees casting long shadows over it. I woke up night after night, drenched in sweat. The image burned into my mind.

Finally, I couldn't ignore the feeling that the dream was trying to tell me something. It was as if a force was guiding me, no, pulling me toward that place. One day, unable to bear the uncertainty any longer, I went to the woods. I didn't tell anyone. I wasn't even sure what I was looking for. But I had to follow my instincts.

The woods were dense. The branches over-head intertwined to block out the sun. I walked deeper and deeper until, after what felt like hours, I found the clearing from my dreams. The sight of it sent chills down my spine.

My heart pounded in my chest as I approached the place from my dreams. In a panic, I dropped to my knees and began digging with my bare hands, the earth cold and unyielding. After several minutes, my fingers raw and bloody, scraped against something hard. I kept going and eventu-ally, to my horror, I uncovered a shallow grave. The reality of what I had found was too much to bear. I vomited.

Then I ran back home blinded by tears. I called my parents who called the police. When everyone arrived, I told them everything I had done and what I feared I found.

After excavating the grave, they confirmed what we feared. It was Sophie.

The next few days were a blur of police questioning. They couldn't understand how I had known where to find her. My explanation of the dreams sounded insane, even to me. I was investigated thoroughly; the police trying to piece together how I could have possibly known how to find my sister's grave.

My parents stood by my side. They never once even hinted that they suspected I'd done something wrong. Yet things between us changed after that. They may have believed I didn't hurt Sophie, but they didn't know how I was able to find her. I think that scared them almost as much.

Added to that was the reaction from the kids at school. They turned on me, whispering behind my back, accusing me of having something to do with Sophie's death. They couldn't fathom how else I would have known where to find her.

Ollie, my best friend since childhood, never once doubted me. She defended me fiercely, shutting down any rumors that came her way. "Jackie didn't do this," she would say. "She found Sophie because she loves her, not because she hurt her."

At home, my grandmother's gentle wisdom, comforted me through the darkest days. "Jackie, you have a gift," she explained. "You feel things others can't. Don't be afraid of it."

The pain of losing Sophie, the changes in how my parents treated me, and being ostracized by my peers left deep scars. But it also shaped me, pushing me towards a path of seeking truth and uncovering the hidden. It was a journey that led me to where I was now, standing in a haunted mansion, trying to solve another young woman's death.

As always, Gabby's presence helped ground me. "It will be okay," she said.

"Thanks for the reminder, Gabby," I murmured, scratching her head. The sound of footsteps snapped me back to the present. Ollie approached, her expression serious. "Jackie, you need to see this."

I took a deep breath, pushing the painful memories aside. "Lead the way," I said.

My always observant friend took my arm and lowered her voice. Her brow furrowed.

"Sis," she whispered, "you okay? You seemed lost in thought and I know..."

Whenever Ollie called me 'sis,' I knew she was serious. I forced a smile.

"I'm fine, Ollie. Just thinking."

"Sophie?"

I swallowed hard, nodding. "Yeah. Sometimes it all comes back, you know?"

She placed a reassuring hand on my shoulder. "Of course it does. What happened with Sophie... it's something no one should ever have to go through. But you found her. You brought her home. That was you, Jackie."

I looked away, the weight of her words pressing down on me. "I just followed my instincts. It wasn't anything special. And yes, we found Sophie, but I've never been able to sense her killer or help figure out what happened to her. I failed."

Ollie shook her head, her grip on my shoulder tightening. "No, you didn't fail. You have a gift, Jackie. You sensed where she was. And maybe you can't control it, or use it whenever it's convenient, or just tap into it on a whim. You still can see and feel things others can't. And we just might need that as we do this job."

I sighed, the memories of high school flooding back. The whispers, the accusations, the way everyone looked at me like I was a monster. "You know how people reacted when I told them about my dreams? They thought I was a freak, or worse, a murderer."

Ollie's eyes softened, filled with the understanding only a genuine friend could offer. "I know it was hard, Jackie. I was there, remember? But you're not in high school anymore. We're adults and you're leading a team of people who trust you and believe in what we're doing here. They deserve to know about your gift. It could help us."

I shook my head, the fear of rejection and suspicion still fresh in my mind. "I can't, Ollie. I can't go through that again. They wouldn't understand."

Ollie sighed, her shoulders sagging slightly. "I get it, Jackie. I really do. But remember, we're all here because we believe in uncovering the truth. And part of that truth is you."

I managed a small smile, touched by her unwavering support. "Thanks, Ollie. Maybe someday... but not now. I need to focus on the task at hand."

She nodded, giving my shoulder a final squeeze before letting go. "Alright. Just know that I'm here for you. Always."

We found the rest of the team gathered around the old papers we had discovered earlier. Ethan and Emily were carefully examining the letters and photographs, their faces serious and intent.

"What did you find?" I asked, stepping closer.

Ethan looked up, his eyes bright with excitement. "These letters... they were written by Margaret Harper, Philip Harper's aunt. She seems to have known quite a bit about the mansion's history and its supposed hauntings."

Emily nodded, her enthusiasm palpable. "And these photographs... they show some rooms in the mansion as they were decades ago. There are even a few with strange shadows and figures in the background."

My interest piqued, I leaned in to get a better look. "This is great! Keep looking."

As Ethan and Emily continued to sift through the letters and photographs from the chest, the musty scent of old paper filled the room, mingling with the faint smell of dust and age, causing everyone to take turns sneezing. Over the sound of sniffles and noses blowing, we heard heavy footsteps echoing down the hallway.

Mia, our producer, came barreling into the room, her presence as subtle as a freight train. She was a skeptic through and through, and as we got closer and closer to starting filming, her disdain became more and more evident. And she had no qualms about letting everyone know exactly how she felt about it.

"Alright, people," Mia announced loudly, her

tone dripping with condescension. "Just checking up on you. How's the ghost hunt going? Found any proof of Casper yet?"

Gabby, perched on a nearby bookshelf, let out an indignant squawk. She took off, swooping down and pecking at Mia's head before flying back up to her perch.

"She's the guy. She's the guy," Gabby squawked a perfect imitation of Adrian Monk.

Mia swatted at Gabby, her face turning red with a mix of embarrassment and anger. "Can you control that bird, Jackie?" she snapped.

I suppressed a grin. "Sorry, Mia. Gabby has a mind of her own."

Mia huffed and crossed her arms. "Anyway, let's get down to business. We're on a tight deadline here. I don't want to pour too much money into this first episode because, quite frankly, I don't expect it to succeed. So, you have until tomorrow morning to find something worthwhile."

"That's not enough time, Mia," I replied, trying to keep my tone even. "We're working hard, but these things take time."

"Well, you have little of that," Mia retorted. "And by the way, to save on costs, you'll be spending the night here. Make yourselves comfortable... if that's possible in this creepy old place."

Gabby, sensing Mia's disdain, mimicked in a

perfect imitation of an old movie villain, "You'll never get away with this!"

Mia shot the parrot a glare. "I'm serious, Jackie. This show is on thin ice. Don't waste my time or money."

With that, she turned on her heel and stormed out of the room, the sound of her footsteps fading into the distance. I let out a breath I hadn't realized I was holding.

"Well, you heard the boss," I said, turning back to the team. "Looks like we're having a sleepover."

Emily, ever the optimist, gave a small smile. "Could be fun, right? Like camping, but with ghosts."

"No big deal," Ollie said. "Leo and I were staying, anyway. We'll share what we brought. I do wish people would stop storming in here and ordering us around, though."

Ethan chuckled. "We'll have to put Gabby on guard."

"Fine by me," Tyler agreed.

I looked around at my team, feeling a sense of camaraderie despite the pressure. "Alright, everyone. Find a spot and get as comfortable as you can. Looks like we're having a sleepover."

The living room of Maplewood Mansion was a stark contrast to its grandeur during the day. The ornate furniture, heavy drapes, and dim lighting gave it an eerie atmosphere.

We set up our makeshift sleeping arrangements. Leo and Emily were on the floor in sleeping bags. Ethan claimed the old, worn couch, and Tyler and Ollie were lounging on settees. I was too restless to sit, so I paced back and forth, my mind racing.

"Alright, let's recap what we've found so far," I said, breaking the silence. "Ethan, Emily, what else did you discover in those letters and photographs?"

Ethan adjusted his glasses and leaned forward, holding a stack of yellowed letters. "These letters were written by Margaret Harper, one of the original residents of the mansion. She was actually born here. She details the strange occurrences and sightings that have plagued this place for well over a century. It seems the hauntings aren't a recent phenomenon."

Emily nodded, her dark eyeliner making her wide eyes stand out even more in the dim light. "And those old photos of the mansion? There are a few with what look like shadows or figures in the background. It's eerie, but it does add credibility to the stories."

I stopped pacing and turned to face the group.

"And Evelyn? What more have we learned about her?"

"As we know, Evelyn was the town's librarian and a bit of an amateur historian," Ethan continued. "Maplewood Mansion fascinated her, and she spent a lot of time researching its history and the rumors of the hauntings. According to her journals and notes, she believed there was something significant hidden in the mansion that could explain the strange sounds and apparitions."

Emily added, "As we know, the police think her murder was the work of someone passing through town, but they never found the killer. Since her death, the hauntings have reportedly gotten worse, scaring away guests and leaving the place practically abandoned. This led some to believe Evelyn's ghost is malicious and evil, possibly even dangerous."

A heavy silence fell over the room as we absorbed the information.

Finally, Tyler broke the silence. "So, what about you guys? Have you ever had any ghostly experiences?"

Leo, who was usually quiet, spoke up first. "When I was a kid, my family lived in this old farmhouse. I used to hear footsteps at night, even though everyone else was asleep. One night, I saw a shadowy figure standing at the end of my bed. I was terrified, but it disappeared when I blinked."

Emily shivered. "That's creepy, Leo. Did you ever see it again?"

"No, just that one time. But it was enough to convince me. What about you?"

"For me, it was during a trip to an old prison. My friends and I were doing a ghost tour for fun. Everyone was laughing and being loud. I felt this icy hand grip my shoulder. I turned around, but no one was there. Everyone thought I was making it up and being dramatic, but it was very real. Ever since then, I've been fascinated by the paranormal. It's like Ethan says, when you realize it's there, you see it everywhere."

Ethan smiled wryly. "Exactly. I've spent my life studying history, and you come across a lot of ghost stories. My first authentic experience was in an old library. I was alone, researching late at night, and I heard whispering. There was no one else there, but the whispers followed me until I left the building. After that, I started intentionally listening for things like that. Then I started to not only hear but also see things. I can't always explain them, but I know they are there."

Ollie nodded thoughtfully, and I wondered what she was going to tell them, considering our shared history.

"I've always been a tech geek," she said, "and one night I was testing some new equipment in an abandoned hospital. I captured a clear EVP that said, 'Help me.' It was the first time I felt like I wasn't alone, and it got me hooked on this stuff. There are some other things, too, but I won't go into it all tonight."

She looked at me and smiled.

Tyler looked uncharacteristically serious. "My grandmother's house was haunted," he said all at once. "She used to tell me stories about a woman in white who would appear at the foot of her bed. I never believed her until I saw the woman myself one night. I never stayed at her place alone after that."

I felt the weight of their stories and knew it was my turn. I looked at Ollie, who nodded. Taking a deep breath, I began. "Okay, you all know about my sister, Sophie, disappearing and then her body being found. Well, what you don't know is that after she disappeared, I started having these vivid dreams that led me to her grave. It was the first time I realized I had this... ability. But the reaction from everyone in school made me keep it to myself for a long time. This team, our show, is the first time I've felt like maybe I could use my gift to help others."

Gabby, perched on a nearby chair, chose that moment to chime in with one of her favorite phrases. "It will be okay!" she squawked, making everyone chuckle.

"Thanks for the reminder, Gabby," I said with a

smile. "We may all have different reasons for being here, but we share a common goal: to uncover the truth."

"How did you know where the grave was?" Emily asked.

"I don't know exactly. It was a sense. A feeling. And it's happened since. Many times. Sometimes it's as simple as finding lost car keys or misplaced glasses. Other times I've had a sense about something that was going to happen, or I would see the news and have a feeling I knew something about whatever the story was."

"Could you help the police?" Leo asked.

My heart leapt into my throat, and I coughed. Without meaning to, Leo had gone straight to my greatest fear. My inability to help the police find Sophie's killer.

"Book 'em, Danno," Gabby said, breaking the silence.

Everyone laughed, and the extra time was exactly what I needed to think. I decided to pretend that Leo was asking about helping the police with other cases, not with Sophie.

"Not really. They don't exactly like this kind of help, as you may have noticed from Detective Ryan's reaction." Everyone laughed gently. "But I can usually insert a clue or a hint and get things pointed in the right direction."

I stopped there and my answer seemed to satisfy everyone.

The room fell silent again, but it was a comfortable silence, filled with understanding and camaraderie. We were a team, bound by our shared experiences and our quest for answers.

"Alright," I said, breaking the silence. "Let's get some rest. Tomorrow is a big day, and we need to be at our best."

I pulled an old sofa closer to the group and laid down. Just as I was closing my eyes, something caught my eye, and I sat bolt upright.

CHAPTER 5

The living room was dim and quiet, the only sound the occasional rustle of sleeping bags and the creak of the old mansion settling around us. The room had turned much colder. It was the kind of cold that seeps so deeply into your bones that a steaming hot bath was the only way to get rid of it.

I blinked, trying to adjust my eyes to the darkness and wondering if I really saw something or it was my imagination.

Then I saw her. In the corner of the room stood a ghostly figure. The faint light from the hallway barely illuminated her. My breath caught in my throat and I instinctively reached for my flashlight, but then thought better of it. I didn't want to shine a bright light into a ghost's eyes. Or through a ghost's eyes.

"Guys? Anyone awake? Are you seeing this?" I said trying not to move my mouth.

I heard several affirmative sounds.

The figure was clearly a woman, dressed in period clothing that looked like it was from over a century ago. She wrung her hands nervously as she flickered in and out of visibility. I hoped the cameras and other equipment were capturing this.

Taking a slow, deep breath, I said, "Hello? Who are you?"

She opened her mouth and then closed it again. Maybe she couldn't speak.

"Are you Evelyn?" I asked. Although her clothing didn't look like something Evelyn would have worn.

She shook her head, confirming my thoughts.

"Can you tell us who you are?"

The figure hesitated, her form shimmering as if she might disappear at any moment. Her lips moved as though she were speaking, but we couldn't hear anything.

She seemed almost fearful and looked around the room frantically. Before I could ask another question, a sudden gust of icy wind swept through the room and she vanished. The temperature slowly rose back up.

"Tell me we got that," I said, turning to Leo, who was already looking at his camera.

"Yeah, we did," he confirmed.

"Sound?" I asked looking at Ollie.

She nodded, her headphones held up to one ear. "Every bit," she confirmed. "But her voice... I need a few. Let me work."

I stood up slowly and stretched. Then I flipped on a light and caught myself as shock and more than a little amusement flooded through me.

Tyler was sitting up on his settee, his hair stuck out in all directions, so he looked like a sleepy hedgehog. Somehow he'd completed his nightly skin care routine with no one noticing, but now he had the remnants of cream smeared down a cheek and what appeared to be tape hanging from his right eyelid.

He caught me staring and smiled.

"It takes a lot to keep this up," he said, gesturing to himself.

I smiled at the irony of it all. Then it hit me how badly I needed to use the bathroom. Between the late hour, the cold, the laughter, and the antici-pation, the urge had come on strong. Just as I was about to excuse myself, Ollie said, "Got it!"

She removed her headphones, and I sat back down and crossed my legs. There was no way I was going to miss this.

Ollie played the snippet a few times, and each time, the voice was a little clearer.

"She's saying 'Lillian,' right?"

Everyone strained to hear as Ollie played the

audio again and again. We could clearly hear me ask, "Who are you?" followed by what sounded like, "Lillian."

"Who is Lillian?" I asked.

Ethan's eyes widened. "Maybe Lillian Moore. Wasn't she a maid who worked at here?" He looked at Emily.

Emily was thumbing through her notes nodding. "Yup. She disappeared under 'mysterious circumstances.'" She made air quotes. "She was here well over a century ago."

"Can you find out more about Lillian and what those mysterious circumstances were?"

"On it!" Emily said. The young woman seemed to have no need for sleep. But to be fair, Ethan was wide awake now, too. After seeing a ghost, and talking to her, I think the adrenaline had us all, if not energetic, at least awake and unlikely to sleep anytime soon.

Despite the late hour, the living room and library buzzed with quiet conversation. After confirming that their gear was operating, Leo and Ollie joined the rest of us as we gathered around Ethan and Emily. They had already catalogued most of the documents and quickly found ones relating to

Lillian's time period and were handing papers back and forth.

Finally, Ethan adjusted his glasses and flipped through a stack of old documents and notes flagged with sticky notes.

"Alright, everyone. Here's what we know so far."

We all leaned in.

"Lillian Moore was indeed a maid for the Harper family. This was around 1850," Ethan began. "From what we've gathered, she was well-liked by the family and the other staff. However, like Emily said, Lillian disappeared under mysterious circumstances. At the time, people assumed she had simply run away, but no one ever heard from her again or could find out where she'd gone."

Ollie frowned. "So she just vanished?"

Ethan nodded. "Back then, it was easy to dismiss a missing servant as someone who had run off to start a new life. There weren't many resources dedicated to finding someone of her standing."

Leo, adjusting his camera equipment to capture the conversation, chimed in. "So, what's the connection, then? Why would Lillian show up when we're here to find out what happened to Evelyn?"

Ethan pulled out a worn notebook that had

belonged to Evelyn. "I have your answer right here! As we know, Evelyn was researching the history of Maplewood Mansion. It seems she also had a visit from Lillian and was equally curious. In her notes, Evelyn says she believes Lillian's disappearance was not a simple case of running away."

He paused for effect, allowing the weight of his words to sink in. "Now, get this. Evelyn says it seems Lillian had fallen in love with someone above her social standing. The notes don't specify who, but it's possible that this relationship could have had something to do with Lillian's disappearance."

"Maybe even murder," Emily added dramatically, her eyes widening.

"And we don't know who the person was?" Tyler asked.

Ethan shook his head. "No. But Evelyn's notes tell us where to keep digging. She herself was close to figuring it out before she was killed. And she even suggests what Emily said. The love affair might have led to her being silenced, either by the Harper family or someone else who felt threatened by the relationship."

"That's how they are connected," Ollie said. "Lillian was murdered because of an affair and Evelyn was murdered because she was close to discovering who killed her!"

Gabby, perched on the back of a chair, chose

that moment to chime in. "The game is afoot!" she squawked.

Everyone smiled, but Gabby was right. These were only theories based on secrets, and we needed a lot more than that.

"Alright everyone, this is a terrific start. Ethan and Emily keep digging. And the rest of us will keep our eyes open for anything that might help."

Ethan nodded, already diving back into his notebook. "We'll keep searching," he said as Emily nodded.

Ollie leaned back, her expression thoughtful. "If Lillian was in love with someone from the Harper family, it could explain a lot. But it also means we need to be careful. Whoever wanted to keep this a secret back then might still be willing to do whatever it takes to protect it."

"Whoever killed Lillian would be long gone by now, though," Leo said.

"True, but obviously someone else wanted to silence Evelyn," Ollie added.

Everyone grew quiet as the implications became even more obvious. We might be in danger.

CHAPTER 6

Tyler Reed: Take 2

The camera opens with a sweeping aerial shot of Maplewood Mansion, its Victorian architecture looming under the cloak of night. The scene transitions to the dimly lit living room where the team is gathered, their faces illuminated by the flickering candlelight.

"Welcome back to 'Haunted Histories.' Tonight, we continue our exploration of Maplewood Mansion, a place steeped in mystery and haunted by the echoes of its past. Our investigation has taken a chilling turn as we encountered a ghostly figure and uncovered a deeper layer of the mansion's dark secrets."

The camera cuts to the ghostly figure of Lillian,

her spectral form captured on camera, standing nervously in the corner of the room.

"Last night, our team witnessed a haunting apparition—Lillian Moore, a maid who served the Harper family over a century ago."

The scene transitions to the team huddled around Ethan as he reads from Evelyn's notes, the dim light casting long shadows on the walls.

"Through painstaking research, historian Ethan Brooks has unearthed Lillian's tragic story. Unlike previous assumptions that she had run away, it now appears Lillian's disappearance was far more sinister. Lillian fell in love with someone above her social standing—a forbidden romance that Evelyn Carter, our town librarian, believed led to her untimely death."

Cut to close-ups of the letters and photographs Ethan and Emily have been examining, revealing glimpses of Lillian's life and her connection to the mansion.

"Evelyn Carter's notes, found among the artifacts in the mansion, suggest she was close to uncovering the truth behind Lillian's fate. Evelyn's meticulous research pointed to a cover-up, hinting that those who felt threatened by Lillian's relationship might have silenced her forever. Evelyn believed that Lillian's disappearance—and probable murder—was not an isolated incident but part of a larger, darker history hidden within the mansion's walls."

The camera pans over the team as they listen to the recordings of Lillian's faint whispers, their faces reflecting a mix of fear and determination.

"Our team is now faced with the daunting task of piecing together these century-old mysteries. Lillian's ghostly visitation was not just a random occurrence; it was a desperate attempt to warn us, to guide us towards the truth that Evelyn was so close to uncovering before her own tragic end."

Tyler's expression grows more intense, his voice lowering to a dramatic whisper.

"As we delve deeper into the shadows of Maplewood Mansion, we must remain vigilant. The secrets we are unearthing have already claimed lives. But we are driven by a relentless pursuit of the truth—a truth that Lillian and Evelyn were silenced for trying to reveal."

The camera zooms in on Tyler's face, capturing his resolute expression.

"Join us as we continue to unravel the haunted histories of Maplewood Mansion. What dark forces have been lurking here for over a century? And who will stop at nothing to keep these secrets buried?"

CHAPTER 7

The first light of dawn was barely breaking through the heavy drapes of Maplewood Mansion when the sound of tires crunching on gravel reached my ears. I rubbed my eyes, still groggy from the restless night and too few hours of sleep, and peeked out the window. A police cruiser had pulled up in front of the mansion, and two officers were making their way to the front door.

"Guys, the police are here," I announced.

Leo, Emily, Ethan, Ollie, and Tyler stirred. The night's events had left us all on edge, and the arrival of the police only added to the unease.

I opened the door just as Detective Ryan and Officer Mitchell approached. They walked past me and entered the living room, their demeanors as unkind and mocking as before. Detective Ryan's eyes swept over the equipment and makeshift sleeping arrangements with a sneer.

"Morning, ghost hunters," he said, his tone dripping with sarcasm. "Find anything that goes bump in the night?"

Before I could respond, Officer Mitchell stepped forward, his expression more curious than disdainful. "Actually, we're here to check in and see if you've made any progress. The chief wants to make sure you're not tearing the place apart."

"We're being careful," I replied, keeping my tone neutral. "And yes, we have found some significant information."

Emily jumped up. "Well, actually, we discovered that Lillian Moore, a maid who worked here over a century ago, might have been murdered. She fell in love with someone above her standing, and we think that might be why she disappeared."

Oh, dear sweet Emily. Why would you tell them that?

Ollie put a hand on Emily's arm. With widened eyes and a quick shake of her head, she stopped her from saying any more.

But the damage had already been done. Detective Ryan rolled his eyes. "A ghost maid in love with a rich guy. Sounds like the plot of a bad romance novel."

"Well, it could be more than that," Ethan interjected, his voice calm but firm. "Evelyn Carter may have discovered this as well. It could have something to do with her murder."

Officer Mitchell looked intrigued. "You think Evelyn was killed because of what she found out about this Lillian Moore?"

"It's possible," I said.

Mitchell glanced at Ryan, who was still smirking. "Maybe we should take this a bit more seriously, Ryan. If there's a connection, it could explain a lot."

Ryan shook his head. "It's already closed. It was someone passing through. There's no evidence of it being anything else. Wrong place, wrong time. Come on, Mitchell. We've wasted enough time here." Then he pointed to me and, for what seemed like the hundredth time, said, "Just don't make a mess."

"Hey, uh, give me a second, okay. Gotta use the bathroom," Mitchell said.

Ryan waved his hand and closed the front door behind him. As soon as the door closed, he turned back to us.

"Look, I don't want to make a big deal about this, but my grandmother knows a lot about the history of this town. She used to work in the historical society and has a ton of old records and documents stuffed away at her house. She might be able to help you."

My interest piqued. "Do you think she would talk to us?"

"I can put you in touch," Mitchell offered. "She loves this kind of thing. Might even enjoy having someone interested in her stories for a change."

Emily's eyes lit up. "That would be amazing. Thank you."

Mitchell nodded and scribbled down a phone number on a piece of paper. "Give her a call. Her name's Clara Mitchell. Just tell her I sent you. And please don't say anything to anyone. My partner wouldn't understand."

After he left, the room fell into a contemplative silence. I held the piece of paper with Mrs. Phillips's number like it was a lifeline. "This could be the breakthrough we need."

The drive to Clara Mitchell's home was filled with quiet anticipation. Ethan, Emily, Leo, and I sat in silence, each lost in our own thoughts. The early morning sun cast long shadows across the road, adding to the eerie feeling that had settled over us since our encounter with Lillian's ghost.

Clara's house was a charming, well-kept cottage on the outskirts of town. Flowers bloomed in the garden, and a white picket fence lined the property, offering a stark contrast to the dark and foreboding atmosphere of Maplewood Mansion. We parked the car and approached the front door, where Clara greeted us with a warm smile.

"Welcome," she said, ushering us inside. "My grandson already told me everything! I'm so glad to meet you. Please, come in and make yourselves comfortable."

We followed her into a cozy living room filled with antiques and family photos. Clara's presence was calming, her warm demeanor a stark contrast to the tension that had followed us from the mansion.

"Thank you for seeing us, Mrs. Mitchell," I said, taking a seat in a comfortable armchair. "We appreciate any help you can give us."

"Call me Clara," she insisted with a smile. "Now, tell me, what have you found so far?"

Ethan took out his notes and explained. "We discovered that Lillian Moore, a maid who worked at Maplewood Mansion over a century ago, disappeared under mysterious circumstances. We also found notes from Evelyn Carter, the town librarian, suggesting that Lillian had an affair with someone from the mansion and may have been killed because of it."

Clara nodded, her eyes reflecting a mix of sadness and curiosity. "Yes, Lillian's story is tragic. She had an affair with someone in the mansion. It was a young man from the Harper family. They were very much in love, but their relationship was forbidden."

Emily leaned forward. "Why?"

"It was thought that Lillian was beneath their status. The Harpers always married money and Lillian, of course, didn't have any."

"Was it so forbidden that Lillian would be sent away?" Ethan asked.

Clara sighed, her expression turning somber. "Well, yes, she was sent away."

"But no one knows where she went. We've looked and looked, but it's like she just disappeared," Emily said.

"There is more to the story, I'm afraid. Hold on, please."

Clara stood up slowly and went to an old wooden desk in the corner of the room. "I pulled these out when I knew you were coming. They belonged to my grandmother, who also worked at the mansion. My grandmother was well-educated and was constantly writing. She kept detailed records of everything that happened in her life... and at the mansion."

We gathered around as Clara spread the diaries and documents on the table.

"This is the section that talks about Lillian and the first time she left the mansion."

"The first time?" I asked.

"Yes, she left twice. The first time to have the

baby, and the second time, well, who knows," Clara sighed.

"A baby! That explains so much," Ethan said. "In that time, it would have been scandalous. Plus, if the father were a Harper, as it seems it was, that would have made it even worse."

Clara nodded as Ethan continued. "So they sent Lillian away to have the child, but she returned afterward. The affair probably picked back up and then she was sent away again."

"Rumors were that she went back to the child, but you can see here that my grandmother didn't believe that. She writes that she believes Lillian was murdered, but there was never any proof. And she wasn't inclined to dig any deeper out of fear for her own life."

"And rightly so. I mean, if Evelyn found this out and she ended up dead, even after all this time. Gosh! Maybe she found out who the baby is! Can you imagine if that child had a child and then that child had a child? It would send the Harper family over the edge!" Emily was standing by now.

Clara's expression grew serious. "Slow down, child. You are saying some very dangerous things right now. You can't accuse the Harpers of anything like that without solid proof, and my grandmother's diary isn't enough. They have a lot of power in this town. And if Evelyn was onto something like that...well, you see what happened to her."

I agreed with Clara. "That would be something for the police, Emily. Let's stay focused on who is haunting the mansion and why. Knowing Lillian's story helps, but I don't think she is the one doing the haunting."

Clara reached out and placed a reassuring hand on Emily's shoulder. "Be careful, all of you. The truth is important, but so is your safety. My grandmother always said that some secrets are buried for a reason."

Emily and Leo worked with Clara and got a few minutes of footage they could use for the documentary. While they were busy, Ethan pulled me aside. "We need to find out more about Lillian's descendants. If we can trace them, we might find out what Evelyn discovered and who wanted to keep it hidden."

"I know and I agree. I'm worried about Emily, though. She's so enthusiastic. She'll spill the beans to anyone and might end up getting herself hurt."

"I'll keep it quiet," Ethan said. "And I'll talk to her."

When the crew finished up, we thanked Clara for her help and gathered the documents she had given us. As we left her cozy cottage and headed back to the mansion, the weight of what we had learned pressed heavily on my mind. The pieces of the puzzle were coming together, but the picture they formed was one of danger and deceit.

Back at Maplewood Mansion, the team gathered in the library, a space now filled with the scent of old books and the hum of our equipment. The tension was palpable as we prepared to discuss what we had learned from Clara Mitchell. The weight of the new information felt heavy, the stakes higher than ever.

I spread out the documents and diaries on the large oak table in the center of the room. "Alright, everyone, let's go over what we know. Clara filled in some crucial gaps about Lillian and the Harper family, but I'm afraid it may have raised more questions than it answered."

The team took their seats around the table, each of them focused and ready to dig deeper. Gabby, perched on a nearby bookshelf, watched us intently, her beady eyes taking in everything.

"We know that Lillian had an affair with someone from the Harper family and had a child," Ethan began, flipping through his notes. "But we need to figure out who the father was. That person could be one of our potential murderers."

"So we decided to focus on the Harper siblings back then. Hopefully, we can establish a timeline and figure out who was around when Lillian was working here," Emily added.

She pulled out a family tree she had been

working on. "From what we've gathered, the Harper family had several children during Lillian's time. There was Charles Harper, the eldest son, who was known to be quite the ladies' man. Then there was Thomas Harper, the younger son, who was more reserved and focused on the family business."

Leo adjusted his camera to capture the family tree. "So, Charles and Thomas are our primary suspects. Either of them could have been involved with Lillian."

Tyler nodded. "But we can't forget about Evelyn. If Lillian's child survived and had a family, there might be someone out there who wants to keep this secret buried and is threatened by the existence of that lineage. They may have harmed Evelyn to keep it a secret."

Ethan tapped his pen on the table, thinking. "Let's consider the descendants. Charles Harper had two children, Margaret and Edward. Margaret never married and moved away, but Edward stayed in town and took over the family business."

Emily added, "Edward had three children: Robert, Anne, and Philip. Robert moved away, Anne stayed in town and married into another prominent family, and Philip inherited the mansion."

I looked at the names on the family tree, trying to piece together the connections. "So Philip

Harper is the current owner of the mansion. He stands to benefit the most from keeping the mansion's reputation intact. If Evelyn discovered something about Lillian's descendants, it could threaten his inheritance and the family's standing."

Ollie nodded. "Exactly. If Lillian's child had descendants, they might have a claim to the mansion. That could explain why someone would go to such lengths to keep it a secret."

Gabby chose that moment to interject, her voice mimicking an old detective show. "Follow the money!"

"Good point, Gabby," I said with a smile. "We need to follow the money and see who benefits the most from the mansion. Philip Harper is definitely a person of interest."

Ethan flipped through Evelyn's notes again. "Evelyn was meticulous in her research. She believed that Lillian's affair and suspected murder were part of a larger cover-up. If she found out about the baby and then was onto who Lillian's descendants are, she might have uncovered a motive for someone to keep that information hidden and a motive for her own murder."

Tyler leaned back in his chair, thinking. "So, we're looking at Philip Harper, but also at anyone else who might stand to gain or lose from the mansion's secrets coming to light. That could include distant relatives or even business partners."

Emily tapped her fingers on the table. "We need to dig deeper into the Harper family history and see if there are any other connections we're missing. Who else might have a reason to keep Lillian's story buried?"

I nodded. "Alright, let's split up the tasks. Ethan and Emily continue to go through Evelyn's notes and see if there's anything we've missed. Ollie and Leo look into the current Harper family and their business dealings. Tyler and I will focus on the mansion itself and see if we can find any hidden documents or clues that might give us more information."

We were deep into our work when the front door of Maplewood Mansion burst open, and Mia stormed in for the second time. Her expression was a mix of irritation and impatience.

"Alright, team," she called out, her voice echoing through the hall. "Time's up. Pack it up and let's go."

"Good grief," Ollie sighed. "Here we go again."

I looked up from the documents I was reviewing with Ethan and Emily. "Mia, we need more time," I said, trying to keep my tone calm.

"We've made significant progress, but there are still too many unanswered questions. One night is simply not enough time. You know this."

Mia rolled her eyes. "One night was the deal. I'm not pouring more money into this wild goose chase."

Gabby, perched on the back of a chair, fluffed her feathers and mimicked in a high-pitched voice, "Wild goose chase! Wild goose chase!"

Mia jumped back and screamed. She covered her head with her hands.

Leo and Ollie exchanged amused glances, trying to suppress their laughter, as Mia shot Gabby a glare.

"Seriously, if you can't shut that bird up, I will."

I sensed the team's reaction to those words. Everyone stopped what they were doing and looked up. Ollie stood, and she and Tyler moved closer to Gabby. No one reacted well to Mia's threat, and she knew it.

"Gabby's just trying to lighten the mood," I said, trying to defuse the tension. "We know you wouldn't hurt her, right?"

Mia nodded, her eyes darting between Tyler and me.

I continued, "But seriously, Mia, we need more time. We've uncovered important information about Lillian Moore and Evelyn Carter. We're close to finding the truth."

Mia crossed her arms, her expression hardening. "I don't care. This show is a waste of resources. You've had time. I want you out of here by noon."

Frustration boiled over. "Mia, no. You can't just pull the plug now. We owe it to Evelyn and Lillian to finish what we started and we owe it to the show to get the full story."

Mia's face turned red with anger. "Look, I'm the producer. What I say goes. Now pack it up and leave, or I'll pull funding from the project altogether and call the police on you for trespassing."

As she turned to leave, I followed close on her heels, my determination unwavering. "Mia, you can't do this. We're so close to uncovering something significant. You can't let your skepticism get in the way."

We argued as we walked down the hall, our voices growing louder with each step. I was vaguely aware of the temperature dropping steadily, but was too focused on stopping Mia.

As we rounded a corner, she stopped short. I ran into her.

She was standing with her hands on her hips now, looking up. A ghostly form took up the entire hallway filling it from the ceiling to the floor.

I recognized the figure of Lillian Moore right away, although this wasn't the same image we'd seen the previous night. This one was radiating an eerie green glow. Her hair and her dress billowed behind her, making her appear larger than she was.

She raised a hand towards Mia's face and she stumbled back as she caught her balance.

"What is this?" Mia demanded. "How are you doing that?"

"It's not us, Mia. It's the ghost of Lillian Harper."

Mia shook her head. "No way. This can't be real." She reached out a hand and ran it through the mist that was Lillian.

"See? It's just a projection or something," she said waving her hand back and forth.

Lillian's ghost drew back and roared. I knew she wouldn't harm Mia, but she seemed intent on scaring her and I was okay with that. She must have been listening to the argument and of course, wanted us to stay. At least I hoped I was interpreting the ghost's motives accurately.

Mia's face went pale, and she looked over her shoulder at me. "W-what is this, really?"

"Lillian, really," I said, my voice steady. "Seems she doesn't want us to leave. She knows you're trying to stop us."

Lillian's form wavered, her eyes locking onto Mia's. Her hand still raised, palm facing Mia as though telling her to stop.

Mia's fear turned to anger, and she clenched her fists. "This is insane. Ghosts aren't real!"

"Then you explain this," I said.

Lillian's form flickered, and jumped, then she lurched towards Mia.

Mia screamed, jumping backwards. "I... I can't explain it." Her hands clawed at mine, but I moved away from her allowing her to experience whatever Lillian had in store for her.

"No, this isn't real. I don't know what you are playing at, but this isn't real."

I put my hand on her arm. "Mia, we need to finish this. Evelyn and Lillian deserve justice. We deserve the chance to find the truth. Just give us more time."

Lillian's ghost roared again and Mia covered her ears.

"Okay, fine. You can have more time. Leave me alone!" Mia rushed past me and ran away.

As Lillian faded away, I said, "Thanks for the help."

I swear she smiled.

CHAPTER 8

"Okay, we've got some more time," I announced to the team. They were staring at the door Mia had run through just moments before.

"What did you do to her?" Ollie asked.

"It wasn't me," I said. "It was Lillian. She convinced Mia to give us some more time."

I didn't explain further, and no one asked any more questions. Instead, we simply got back to work.

While everyone else was busy, I kept feeling drawn back to the basement. I also wanted to explore some more on my own, without the team. I still wasn't ready to fully use my so called 'gifts' with these investigations and even if I did, I doubted anyone would listen to me. Considering the reactions from the police all those years ago, and then just today, I decided to keep my feelings to myself.

"I'm going to walk around the house some more," I said. "See what I can find."

"Want some company?" Ollie asked. She had one eyebrow raised in a knowing way.

"No, thanks. I'm good. I've got Gabby for company."

"Okay, then. We'll carry on here. Be careful."

As Gabby and I headed to the basement, Gabby began to softly whistle "Carry on My Wayward Son," by Kansas. Ollie's comment about the team carrying on must have put it in her mind.

Wishing I had the team from *Supernatural* with me, I entered the basement with Gabby firmly perched on my shoulder, still whistling softly. We'd barely explored this area the last time we were down here. After finding all the letters and photos, everyone was so excited that we never got around to really diving into the room's secrets and treasures. I couldn't shake the feeling that I was being watched, and I hoped it was Lillian or Evelyn watching over me. It didn't feel like that, though.

Suddenly Gabby stopped whistling and flapped her wings. She flew off ahead of me, deeper into the basement. "Gabby, where are you going?" I called after her, my voice echoing off the stone walls.

She landed near a section of the wall that looked slightly different from the rest. "It's showtime!" She said, spreading her wings.

I ran my fingers along the edge of the wall where Gabby was standing, feeling for any gaps or irregularities. Suddenly, the wall gave way, revealing a narrow passage.

"Good eye, Gabby," I said.

I debated exploring the passage by myself. On the one hand, no one knew about it except me, so if something happened, I'd likely be stuck for a while. On the other hand, it was just a room in an old house. My gut told me it would be okay, and I squeezed through the entrance.

I found myself in a small room. The air was musty, and the room was filled with old furniture and boxes covered in dust.

Gabby joined me, her head bobbing up and down and her tail feathers spread as though she were ready to fly away.

I rummaged around a bit but only found old dishes and linens packed away in crumbling boxes. I sneezed.

"There's nothing here, Gabby," I said. "Just a storage room."

"Gotta scoot," Gabby said, still bobbing up and down. She was obviously nervous being in the small enclosed room.

"Okay, we can go. But you know, if there are

rooms like this in the basement, it makes me wonder what the attic is like."

Gabby didn't answer as I squeezed back through the narrow opening and into the larger basement area.

"Just one more second," I murmured to myself as I walked the perimeter of the room looking for any more secret passageways. Suddenly a series of loud thuds coming from above my head broke my concentration. I thought I heard yelling as well.

Gabby took off, and I followed closely behind her.

When I got back to the main floor, there was complete chaos. Tyler was holding Leo upright, his right arm over his shoulders as Leo's head bobbed and dripped blood.

"Oh, my gosh! What happened!"

"Leo was attacked. Someone broke in and Leo went after him. We have to get to the hospital," Ollie said as she held a towel to Leo's head. "Come on."

"We'll stay behind and clean up," Ethan said.

"Call us as soon as you know something," Emily added.

Ollie drove like a maniac while Tyler called the

police. Soon we had Leo in the ER and were sitting in the waiting room while they wheeled him away.

"I heard what you told the police in the van," I began. "But now tell me what really happened," I said as we settled in. Now that the panic was over, and I knew Leo was being cared for, I wanted the details.

Ollie began. "We were all in the library and Leo was in the living room. He said he wanted to adjust the camera that picked up Lillian last night just in case she showed up again. And he was irritated that he didn't get Lillian's interactions with Mia and was planning to set up a camera in the hallway too."

Tyler continued. "So we were all working, doing our things and we heard Leo yell out. Then we heard a series of loud thuds and bangs."

I nodded, remembering the sounds I heard from the basement.

"We all ran into the living room and saw someone going through one of the French windows. Leo was right on his tail."

"Tyler didn't even hesitate," Ollie added. "He ran after them, too. Then they both came back, Leo dripping blood everywhere."

"Yeah, the intruder had some sort of metal stick, I guess like a fire poker or something like that. Just before Leo caught him, he stopped and swung it towards his head. Leo went down right away, and I stopped chasing him to help Leo. That was an awful lot of blood," Tyler said.

"And whoever it was, destroyed a fair amount of equipment," Ollie added. "They must have used the metal poker to break things. Monitors are busted and cameras are cracked."

I listened to Tyler and Ollie relate what happened, and my heart sank. We were officially in over our heads. Someone was seriously injured and our equipment was destroyed. There was no way Mia was going to pay to replace anything.

I felt a wave of guilt wash over me. I had brought everyone here, convinced that we could uncover the truth with no real danger. Now Leo was hurt, and we were all at risk.

"Stop it," Ollie said.

I looked at her. "What?"

"Sis..."

"Ollie..."

"No, I mean it, Jackie. I know exactly where your mind is going right now, and I'm telling you to stop it. This wasn't your fault. You couldn't have known this would happen and there's no way you could have stopped it. So stop the pity party you are getting ready to throw. Just stop it."

Tyler's eyes grew wide. "Yeah, uh, Jackie, I don't know you that well, but, yeah, there's no reason for you to feel bad about this. I mean, how could you possibly be responsible for this? Leo's an adult, we all are. We know the risks of what we do."

They were both right, and I knew it. Granted, Tyler was kinder in his encouragement, but they were right.

"Okay," I finally said, if for no other reason than to make them shut up. "I'm fine. No guilt or anything. I just really hate what happened, you know?"

We sat in silence for several moments while I hoped that was the end of the pep talk. I felt guilty. Nothing was going to change that. And I was seriously considering calling the entire thing off. But I didn't want to hear what I knew to be the truth. It didn't change anything.

Thankfully, the nurse wheeled poor Leo out to us before Ollie or Tyler could say anything else.

"All done," she said. "You can take him home. He has stitches and meds for pain. Plus a likely concussion, so here is a sheet on the protocol you need to follow for the next forty-eight hours. Will someone be able to stay with him?"

We all nodded.

"Absolutely," I said.

While Ollie got the van, Tyler and I got more instructions and Leo sat with a half smile on his face.

"How you doing, buddy?" Tyler asked him.

Leo gave a thumbs up and then got distracted

by his own hand. He turned it over and looked at his palm, then back to his knuckles.

The nurse chuckled. "Pain meds. We don't want to knock him out, but he needed something. He's going to have one heck of a headache when everything wears off."

Ollie arrived out front with the van and we loaded Leo in. I sent a text to Ethan, letting them know Leo was okay, and we were on our way back.

When we arrived at the mansion, Emily had found a recliner in one of the guest rooms, and she and Ethan had moved it into the library.

We guided Leo to it and settled him in. After telling Ethan and Emily what the nurse had said, we turned our conversation to other issues.

I said what I'd been thinking at the hospital. "I'm sorry," I said, my voice barely a whisper. "I never wanted anyone to get hurt. Maybe... maybe we should call this off."

"No way," Leo slurred. "We're too close to the truth to back down now."

"Leo, you are injured," I began.

"So? I'm okay. I'll heal. But Lillian and Evelyn? They won't."

"Exactly," Ethan said. "We're too close to the truth to back down now. And now that we know what we're up against, we'll just need to be smarter and more cautious."

Ollie nodded, her expression grim. "Right. We can't let our guard down."

"This isn't your fault, Jackie. We all knew there were risks. We just need to stick together and keep pushing forward," Emily added.

Even Gabby felt the need to chime in. "Who you gonna call?" She said.

I took a deep breath, trying to steady my nerves. "Okay. But we need to be more vigilant. Let's double-check all our equipment and set up some security measures. We have to take care of ourselves. The police never even showed up after Tyler's report, so it's on us to make sure this doesn't happen again."

Ethan nodded. "I'll see if we can find any security cameras or alarms we can set up. We need to know if anyone tries to break in again."

Tyler placed a reassuring hand on my shoulder. "We're in this together, Jackie. We'll get through it."

With renewed determination, we set to work, reinforcing our defenses while taking turns making sure Leo could be woken up every few hours. The attack had left us shaken, but it had also strengthened our resolve. Whoever was trying to stop us had made a mistake—they had underestimated our commitment to uncovering the truth.

"Bingo!"

Ollie's exuberance was unexpected in the quiet room and made all of us jump.

"Geez, Ollie! You scared me," I said, trying to bring my heart rate back down.

"Sorry, but look what I found."

As we crowded around, she pressed play. We watched, amazed as somehow she had managed to splice together snippets of video saved from the disaster. While the image was somewhat grainy, we could clearly see the timestamp was shortly before Leo was attacked.

At first, it was just the usual creaks and shadows of the old mansion. But then, a figure appeared on the screen behind Leo. We could see the figure as he realized someone was in the room. He seemed to hesitate, then pulled a hood over his head before he began destroying the equipment.

We saw Leo jump up and go after the intruder, then Tyler appeared and they chased him through the French doors.

"Wait," Ollie said. "Watch and look closely." She rewound the video back to when the intruder first appeared.

We all leaned in and my heart skipped a beat. It was the family attorney, Bob Lawson. His face was clearly visible for a moment before he covered it.

"It's him," Leo said, his voice a mix of disbelief and anger. "He's the one who attacked me."

I nodded, my mind racing. "We need to call the police again. This proves that someone's trying to stop us, and now we know who it is."

Ollie grabbed her phone and dialed 911, explaining the situation to the dispatcher and demanding a police response. Within minutes, we heard sirens approaching the mansion.

Of course, Detective Ryan and Officer Mitchell were the ones to arrive. They listened as we explained what had happened.

"Yes, we know. We got the report at the station," Officer Ryan said.

"But look what we found," Ollie said and showed them the video evidence.

As he watched, Ryan's expression grew grim. "Okay, folks. This changes things. If Bob Lawson is involved, there's more at stake here than we realized."

Mitchell nodded, his face serious. "We'll bring him in for questioning. In the meantime, you all need to be careful. If Lawson will go this far, there's no telling what else he might do."

Ryan looked at me, his tone softer than before. "You did good finding this. But now, we need to make sure you're all safe. We'll have an officer posted here to monitor things."

As the police began their investigation, I felt a

mix of relief and apprehension. We had uncovered a crucial piece of the puzzle, but the danger was far from over. Bob Lawson was trying to stop us, and now we had proof.

~

The atmosphere in Maplewood Mansion was heavy with anticipation as we waited to hear from the officers. We wondered if Bob Lawson was still out there and if he would try something again. It was comforting to know an officer stood guard on the front porch, but Lawson had broken in through a French door on the side of the house so obviously, if someone wanted to get in without alerting the guard, they could.

When Detective Ryan and Officer Mitchell finally returned, their expressions were unreadable. We gathered in the library, eager to hear what they had to say.

Ryan cleared his throat, looking at each of us. "We spoke with Bob Lawson. He claims he was here to supervise your activities, but you refused to let him in. He says he 'broke in' only because he has every right to be here as the Harper family's attorney."

"That's ridiculous," Tyler snapped, his frustration clear. "He wasn't supervising. He was destroying our equipment!"

"And wearing a hood so he couldn't be identified," Emily added. "Explain that!"

Mitchell held up a hand. "We understand your frustration, but from a legal standpoint, Lawson's explanation holds up. He has a right to be here, and without concrete evidence of malicious intent, we can't arrest him."

Ollie shook her head in disbelief. "Evidence of malicious intent? How about Leo's poor head? If that's not malicious, I don't know what is!"

Ryan sighed. "He said he was afraid and was defending himself because you guys were chasing him."

The frustration and outrage in the room was palpable. I clenched my fists, trying to keep my anger in check.

"Look, I know how you feel. And we aren't stupid, despite what you might think. We'll keep an eye on Lawson. And here are our private numbers. If you need anything, if something else happens, call and we'll take action." Ryan handed me his card.

Through clenched teeth, I thanked them both and walked them to the door. Without another word, I closed the door behind them and turned back to the team.

"Lawson has just made himself our number one suspect for Evelyn's murder. We need to keep digging and find proof that ties him to her death."

Emily nodded, her eyes filled with determination. "We can't let him get away with this. Evelyn deserves justice, and so does Lillian."

I took a deep breath and looked around at my team. "Alright, let's regroup. If anyone wants to leave, it is perfectly okay to do so. This has taken a dangerous turn. Ghosts are one thing, but now we know we're dealing with a killer. Leo, I promise, no one would think any less of you and you can join us for the next show."

Leo laughed. "Nope. Sorry. Not going anywhere!"

"Anyone else?" I asked. "No harm, no bad feelings. I really mean it."

Everyone stood watching me and not saying a word.

"Alright then! Let's double-check everything we've found so far and see if there's anything we missed. We can't let Lawson intimidate us into giving up."

Leo, despite his injury, managed a determined smile. "We've come this far. We can't back down now."

Tyler agreed. "Yeah, Lawson may think he's won, but we're not done yet."

CHAPTER 9

Tyler Reed: Take 3

The camera opens with a sweeping aerial shot of Maplewood Mansion, its Victorian architecture looming under the cloak of night. The scene transitions to the dimly lit library where the team is gathered, their faces illuminated by the flickering candlelight. Tyler Reed steps into view, his expression grave and focused, ready to narrate the latest developments in their investigation.

"Good evening, viewers. I'm Tyler Reed, and welcome back to 'Haunted Histories.' Tonight, we continue our journey into the shadows of Maplewood Mansion, uncovering secrets long buried and facing dangers that have been hidden for over a century. Our investigation has taken a turn, both chilling and revealing."

The camera cuts to a cozy living room where Jackie, Ethan, and Emily are seated across from an elderly woman, Clara Mitchell. The scene shifts to show snippets of their conversation.

"Earlier today, we visited Clara Mitchell, a local historian with deep ties to the mansion's past."

The camera shifts onto Clara. "Lillian Moore's story is tragic. She was a young maid who served the Harper family in the mid 1800s. Poor Lillian's life was marked by a forbidden romance with a member of the Harper family. And it lead to the birth of a child."

The screen shows a close-up of Clara's hands as she hands over old diaries and documents to Jackie and Ethan.

"Clara provided us with invaluable documents, including diaries and letters from that era. These records reveal that Lillian went away to have her child in secret, returning to the mansion only to disappear again a few months later. The official story was that she left to reunite with her child, but whispers of foul play have persisted for decades."

The scene transitions to the team back at the mansion, their faces lit by the glow of computer screens as they review the footage from the break-in.

"Our investigation took a dangerous turn when an unknown assailant broke into the mansion, destroying our equipment and leaving one of our team members injured. Thanks to quick thinking and our surveillance cameras, we identified the intruder as Bob Lawson, the Harper family's attorney."

The camera shows the grainy footage of Bob Lawson pulling a hood over his head before beginning his destructive rampage.

"Lawson claimed he was only here to supervise our activities, but the video evidence tells a different story. His actions raise serious questions about his motives and his possible involvement in both Lillian's disappearance and Evelyn Carter's murder."

The scene shifts to the police arriving at the mansion, discussing the situation with Jackie and the team.

"Despite the clear evidence of sabotage, the police were unable to take immediate action against Lawson, citing his legal right to be on the property. This setback has only strengthened our resolve to uncover the truth."

The camera returns to Tyler, standing in the dimly lit library, his expression determined.

"As we press on with our investigation, the stakes have never been higher. We are not only seeking justice for Evelyn Carter and Lillian Moore, but also protecting ourselves from those who wish to keep these dark secrets buried."

CHAPTER 10

"Hey, got a minute?"

Ollie sat down next to where Tyler and I were working on his script for the next voice-over.

"Sure," I said.

"Want privacy?" Tyler asked, preparing to get up from the table and hitting his knee on the leg. "Ouch."

"Nope, you need to be in on this, too."

Tyler sat back down and my blood turned cold. When Ollie used words like 'in on this,' you could be confident something major was getting ready to go down.

"Ollie?" I said with what I hoped was a warning behind my voice.

Apparently, if there was a warning, Ollie decided to ignore it.

"We need to invite Bob Lawson here," she said.

"What? Are you kidding me? After what he did, invite him back?" I was actually grateful that Tyler was sitting there hearing all of this so that I'd have backup. No one in their right mind would think this was a good idea.

"Yeah, I like it," Tyler said.

Okay, so he's not in his right mind.

Ollie held up a hand and fluttered it in my face, as though that gesture would do any good at all. "Now, wait before you freak out. I have a plan and it really could work."

"Let's hear it," Tyler, again being helpful, said.

"Sure, fine," I said the words, but I didn't mean them.

"We know he was here. We know the police interrogated him and we know he lied. So let's confront him. Let's see what he has to say for himself to us. It's just possible he tells us something that will further incriminate him," Ollie added.

"Or further injures us," I deadpanned.

"Yes, that's brilliant! We can get him here by telling him we want to interview him. I'll do it. Leo still can't use equipment, but Ollie can run the camera, right?"

Ollie nodded.

"And if we're all there, what's he going to do? He'll be on camera so everything is being taped.

We can even set it up so the feed goes to backups. That way, if anything happens, someone will get the video. Maybe Mia?"

Tyler couldn't even say that last part with a straight face and Ollie and I laughed along, enjoying his joke. Of course, we couldn't use Mia. But there were others at the station who would keep the confidence and the video.

I sat back and thought it through. They both made a good point. We'd have to let him know up front that every second he was in the house he would be recorded to an off-site backup. That way, when we confronted him, he wouldn't suddenly turn violent. It just might work.

"Okay, if for no other reason than to get more footage. He is someone we should interview anyway, so...okay. But let's make sure everyone else is okay with it, too. I don't want to upset Leo or-"

"Leo is just fine," Leo said from the doorway where he stood with the rest of the team.

"We all are just fine," Emily added and clapped her hands. "Operation Confrontation is a go!" She sang as she literally skipped away, her heavy, black boots making loud thumps across the wooden floors.

I shook my head at Ollie.

"The truth is out there!" Gabby squawked happily from her perch.

"Oh, Gabby, not you too?"

"Good afternoon," Bob Lawson said as he stepped into the library. "What can I help you with?"

I took a deep breath, trying to steady my nerves. "Thank you for coming, Mr. Lawson. Especially on such short notice. We realized we needed to interview you for the show. You are obviously highly invested in what we're doing here, so we wanted to include you."

Lawson raised an eyebrow, his expression curious but cautious.

"Before we begin, you need to know that you are being recorded and everything you say and do is being uploaded to an off-site location. If anything happens to us, the person receiving the transmission will immediately notify the police," Ethan said.

"Okay," Lawson looked confused.

Then Ethan held up a tablet with the video footage queued up. "Yes, despite the video evidence of you breaking into the mansion and destroying our equipment, we still thought you deserved to have your say." He pressed play and watched triumphantly as our evidence was displayed.

Lawson's face, however, remained impassive as he watched the video. When it finished, he looked up, his expression unreadable. "I already explained to the police. I was here to supervise and ensure you weren't damaging the property. You refused to let me in, so I had no choice but to enter on my own."

Emily crossed her arms, her voice firm. "Supervision doesn't involve destroying equipment, Mr. Lawson. We believe you were trying to sabotage our investigation."

Lawson sighed, rubbing his temples. "I understand how this looks, but I had no malicious intent. I was frustrated and acted impulsively. But sabotage? That's a serious accusation."

I stepped forward, meeting his gaze. "How about assault? How's that for an accusation? You know good and well Leo wasn't chasing you to do harm, and yet you could have killed him."

His face changed and crumbled. "I am so sorry about that. That was never my intent. I didn't realize how close he was to me or I never would have swung like that. How is he, if I may ask? And I would like to apologize to him personally."

That threw us all off, and I literally stumbled and stuttered over my next words.

"Um, sure, yeah, that would be good. I mean, he's okay. Well, a concussion and a heck of a lump on his head, but...Mr. Lawson, we called you here because we believe you had a motive to stop us. We think you murdered Evelyn Carter to protect yourself and the mansion. And we are fairly confident that there's a financial reason behind it."

For a moment, Lawson's expression hardened, but he quickly regained his composure. "Financial reason? That's absurd. I have no financial interest in this mansion beyond my legal duties to the Harper family."

Ollie leaned in, her voice sharp. "Then why go to such lengths to interfere with our work?"

Lawson shook his head. "You have it all wrong. I was angry because I felt you were meddling in things that could tarnish the Harper family's reputation, sure. But financial gain? That's not it."

Tyler, who had been observing quietly, finally spoke. "If it's not about money, then what is it about? What do you think we'll find that would tarnish their reputation? Why are you so determined to stop us?"

Lawson took a deep breath, looking genuinely weary. "The Harper family has a long and complicated history. There are secrets that, if revealed, could hurt many people. My job is to protect the family's interests, but that doesn't include murder or injury," he added.

I watched his face closely, trying to gauge his sincerity. "So, you're saying you had nothing to do with Evelyn's death?"

Lawson met my gaze steadily. "I had nothing to

do with Evelyn's death. I have an alibi for the night she was killed, and you can verify it. I was attending a conference out of town, surrounded by colleagues who can vouch for me."

Emily frowned. "Then who would have motive to kill Evelyn and try to stop us?"

Lawson sighed again. "I don't know. But if you're serious about uncovering the truth, you'll need to look beyond me. The Harper family's history is full of people who had motives, secrets, and opportunities."

We exchanged glances, unsure of what to believe. Lawson's calm demeanor and confident alibi left us at a crossroads.

"Alright," I said finally. "We'll verify your alibi. But know this, Mr. Lawson, we won't stop until we find out who killed Evelyn and what happened to Lillian."

Lawson nodded, looking relieved but still wary. "I understand. I just hope you find the truth without causing more harm."

"Trust me, so do I," I said.

As Bob Lawson was preparing to leave after his interview, he hesitated at the door, his face conflicted. He seemed to wrestle with an internal decision before finally turning back to us.

"Wait," Lawson said, his voice breaking the tense silence. "There's more that I didn't tell you. If you're serious about finding the truth, there's something you need to know. Can we talk outside? I don't want it known that this came from me and I absolutely do not want this recorded."

We exchanged cautious glances before agreeing to follow Phillip Lawson outside.

The entire team surrounded him as he spoke, his voice filled with a mixture of frustration and resignation.

"As you know, Philip Harper is the current owner of Maplewood Mansion, and the one who brought you all here," Lawson explained. "On the surface, he appears to be the respectable head of the Harper family, dedicated to preserving the family legacy. But there's more to him than meets the eye."

"We didn't think he was a suspect in Evelyn's murder since he literally hired us to figure out what happened to her," I said.

"Exactly," Lawson confirmed. "He covers his tracks very well."

Ollie narrowed her eyes. "What do you mean?"

Lawson looked at each of us. "Philip stands to lose the most if the secrets of the mansion come to light. The Harpers' wealth and status are built on a carefully maintained facade. If Lillian's descendants were to come forward with a claim to the mansion, it would cause a scandal that could destroy everything Philip has worked to protect."

Emily leaned in, her curiosity piqued. "So, you're saying Philip had a motive to stop Evelyn from uncovering the truth about Lillian and her descendants?"

"Exactly," Lawson said, nodding. "The fact that Lillian had a child is well known within the family. What isn't known is who those descendants are. And, yes, they've looked. Names were changed, identities hidden, even the Harper money couldn't uncover the lineage. But apparently Evelyn had found something, and I suspect she made the mistake of sharing it with Philip. If she indeed found proof of Lillian's descendants and their connection to the Harper family, it could have jeopardized his inheritance and the mansion's future."

Tyler crossed his arms, his expression skeptical. "But what about the financial motive? Does Philip stand to gain financially from keeping these secrets hidden?"

Lawson sighed. "The Harper family's wealth is tied to the mansion and its historical significance. If the truth about Lillian and her descendants were to come out, it could lead to legal battles over the property and damage the family's reputation and ultimately their financial hold over the town. Philip is determined to avoid that at all costs."

Ethan's brow furrowed in concentration. "So, Philip had both a personal and financial motive to stop Evelyn. But does he have an alibi for the night she was killed?"

Lawson shook his head. "I'm sure I don't know. But I will say Philip is careful, and he has the resources to cover his tracks." He turned to Leo and extended his hand. "Once again, young man, I am so terribly sorry. I do hope you heal quickly."

Leo shook his hand and nodded. There wasn't much else to say.

As Bob Lawson drove away, we wandered back into the mansion.

Ethan said, "Lawson might not be the killer, but he's right about one thing—the Harper family's history is full of secrets."

"Agreed," I said. "Let's verify his alibi first. I have a feeling he's telling the truth, but I'm not willing to let him off the hook just yet. And as far as Philip goes, we have a lot of work to do."

The team went back inside, but something was nagging at the back of my mind.

"I'm going to walk around a little," I said. "I want to think some things through."

As they walked away, Gabby did her best Columbo imitation and said, "Just one more thing."

"I know Gabby, but what?"

She didn't have an answer for me, but I found

myself wandering around the back of the mansion. Something out here was calling to me. That gift, those instincts, whatever you want to call them, were pulling me ....pulling me somewhere. I didn't know where, but somewhere.

CHAPTER 11

The mansion was eerily quiet as I sat alone in the library. Wandering through the back-yard of the mansion hadn't revealed anything, and the weight of the investigation was pressing down on me. The flickering candlelight cast long shadows on the walls, adding to my feelings of isolation. The rest of the team was resting or working in other parts of the mansion, leaving me with my thoughts and doubts.

I missed my grandmother. She had always known what to say to lift my spirits and guide me through tough times. Now, with Leo injured and the investigation growing more dangerous, I felt the burden of responsibility more than ever.

Gabby, perched on a nearby bookshelf, seemed to sense my unease. She fluttered down to the table and looked at me with her keen, intelligent eyes. "It will be okay," she squawked, her voice mimicking my grandmother's comforting tone.

I couldn't help but smile, despite my worries. "Thanks, Gabby," I said softly. "I wish I could believe that."

The parrot tilted her head, as if studying me. "It will be okay," she repeated, more insistent this time.

I sighed, running a hand through my hair. "You know, I could really use some of that psychic energy I supposedly have," I said sardonically, looking at Gabby. "Any chance you can channel Grandma for me and tell me what to do next?"

Gabby fluffed her feathers and let out a series of clicks and whistles, her version of a laugh. "It's a gift and a curse," she added.

I laughed despite myself. My tension eased slightly. "Yeah, Monk, again. Right? This is a gift and a curse. Seriously, Gabby, how do I keep everyone safe and figure this all out at the same time?"

Gabby didn't answer, of course. She just looked at me with those wise eyes, as if she understood more than she let on. I reached out and gently scratched her head, finding some comfort in her presence.

"Thanks for being here," I murmured. "I know it's silly, but you sure do help."

The quiet of the mansion seemed to press in

on me again, but Gabby's presence was a reminder that I wasn't completely alone. My team was here, and they believed in me. And somewhere, I hoped, my grandmother was watching over us.

"Okay, Gabby," I said, standing up and squaring my shoulders. "Let's get back to work. We have a mystery to solve."

Gabby flapped her wings and squawked, "We've got work to do!"

I was about to agree with Gabby when something caught the corner of my eye.

It began as a flutter, a sort of waviness in the air. Then as I focused, the image solidified into first one, then a second form. My heart was pounding, although really, I should be getting used to this. Within moments, Lillian and what I assumed to be Evelyn appeared side by side, their forms shimmering and barely visible in the dim light.

"Hi guys," I whispered, my voice trembling. "What's up?"

The two spirits struggled to communicate, their forms flickering as they tried to convey their message. It was as if they were caught between worlds, their voices barely more than whispers carried on the cold air.

I shot a quick glance towards the cameras and

confirmed they were running. Hopefully, they would pick this up.

I took a deep breath and focused, trying to catch the faint words they were saying. Evelyn's mouth moved, but the sound was distorted, like a voice carried from a great distance.

"Wrong place," Evelyn whispered, her voice barely audible.

Lillian's form flickered violently, her eyes wide with urgency. "Not him," she said, her voice echoing with a desperate plea.

I furrowed my brow, trying to understand. "Wrong place? Not him? Not Bob Lawson? Right, we figured."

Evelyn nodded slowly, her gaze intense. "Look... elsewhere," she said, her voice gaining a little more clarity.

"We did, we are. We're looking at Phillip Harper," I said, trying to stay calm.

Lillian stepped forward, her hand reaching out towards me, though it passed through the air like mist. "Harper... family," she said, her voice trembling with emotion.

I nodded, piecing together their message. "That's what we think. That it's someone in the Harper family. That's where we're looking."

Evelyn and Lillian exchanged a glance, their forms shimmering in the cold air. They nodded in unison, their expressions a mix of relief and urgency.

"Secrets," Evelyn whispered.

"Not here," Lillian repeated, her voice a haunting whisper.

I took a deep breath, feeling the weight of their message settle over me. "Okay," I said, my voice steady. "We'll look beyond the obvious suspects, focusing on the Harper family. And not here. I don't know what that means. Not here at the mansion?"

The two spirits began to fade, their forms becoming more insubstantial by the second. The air turned bitterly cold and a steady breeze blew despite no windows being opened. The poker by the fireplace began to rattle, sounding like chains being dragged across a floor.

"Wait! Tell me more about 'not here.' What do you mean?"

They both looked frightened, their eyes darting all over the room, then Lillian disappeared completely, with Evelyn close behind her.

"Wait, Evelyn, what do you mean?"

Evelyn gave me one last look and pointed upwards, then she was gone as well.

The chill in the air slowly dissipated.

I sat there for a moment, absorbing what had just happened. The ghosts of Evelyn and Lillian had guided me away from Bob Lawson and Phillip

Harper, showing that we needed to look deeper. They seemed to confirm it was someone in the Harper family though, who else was left?

And what did they mean by 'not here'?

"Okay, Gabby," I said. "Let's go find the others and tell them what we've learned."

But before I could turn, the rest of the team was already coming in.

"We got an alert!" Emily said.

"And we picked up the entire thing," Leo exclaimed. He wasn't supposed to be looking at monitors yet, but the look on his face was so happy and excited, I wasn't going to fuss at him.

We gathered around the monitors as usual and watched over and over as barely visible images fluttered before me.

"I hate this. It could be a trick of the camera, or the light. Why is it they never appear on video like they do to the naked eye?" I groused.

"I know. It would be so much easier to prove all this. The debunkers will have a field day with this video," Leo said. "I can't clean it up any more without losing them altogether."

"And you shouldn't even be doing that much, right?" Ollie was playing mom, so I didn't have to.

"Move over, kid. Let me take the reins. Close your eyes and rest. I'll ask questions if I need you."

Leo pouted, but he did as he was told. I saw him rubbing his temples as he sat down away from the monitors. He still wasn't okay and, according to Dr. Google, he wouldn't be for a few more days at least. We had to be vigilant.

"Let's put aside the issue of the quality of video for now and concentrate on what their message was. Ollie, how is the sound?" Ethan asked.

"Decent," she said. "You can catch some of the phrases and knowing what they actually said helps. See? Right here," she played a snippet of the recording, "you can hear one of them say 'not here' and then rewind a little bit more and you can hear this." She replayed the audio, and we caught the beginning of the interaction where they told me "wrong place."

Ollie looked at me. "Anything else? Did they say anything else that you heard, but the audio didn't get?"

I shook my head. "No, that was it. Oh, and Evelyn pointed up just before she disappeared. Can you see that on video? It's just after I asked her what she meant by 'not here' at the very end."

Ollie shook her head. "No, the image isn't clear enough to see her hands, much less a finger pointing. And she didn't say anything either, correct?"

"Correct," I confirmed.

This was getting frustrating. Obviously, appearing like that was difficult for them and communicating was even harder. They went to the effort to show up and speak, but I couldn't make sense of what they were telling me.

We already knew to look beyond Bob Lawson, and they were even saying to look beyond Phillip Harper. Great. According to the family tree, that only left about twenty people to look at. And 'not here?' What the heck was I supposed to do about that little nugget? Not the mansion? Not Maplewood? Where then?

"I need a break," I said, pushing back my chair and standing.

Ethan and Ollie stood with me, and Ollie grabbed my hand.

"Are you okay?" She asked.

"Yeah, I just want to be alone. Think."

I felt like my skin was crawling and didn't want to be touched. I was also tired of talking and overwhelmingly irritated. Something was going on, but all I wanted was to be left alone. I bit my tongue to keep from snapping at Ethan and Ollie as they looked at me with so much concern. They were just trying to help, but I wanted to throat punch them.

I am self-aware enough to know when it's me, and in this case, it definitely was all me. Something was off. I took a deep breath.

"Look, I'm just feeling off. I'm okay, but I really need to be alone. Please, just give me some space."

"Okay," Ollie said. "Call if you need anything." And being the amazing friend she is, she distracted Ethan, and they both went back to reviewing the video. No one else seemed to notice the interaction, so I was free to leave.

I tapped my shoulder, and Gabby arrived quickly. She also had enough sense to keep her beak closed.

I decided to go upstairs and just wander the hallways. We had monitors and cameras up there, at least one in each room, but we had zero activity from any of them. The library and living area were the most active. Probably that's where Lillian was killed, and we knew it's where Evelyn died.

When I reached the top step, I leaned against the wall and took several deep breaths. Whatever was going on downstairs was dissipating and I was feeling more like myself. I'd spent an awful lot of time by myself, which was unusual, especially during a shoot. Something was off.

"Probably a hot flash or something," I muttered. "Hormones running amok."

"Amok, amok, amok!" Gabby said, followed by her clicking sounds.

I laughed with her, and my shoulders relaxed. As my breathing settled, I wandered around the hallways, just looking at the portraits that hung on the walls and absorbing the energy and history of the place.

"Okay, Grandma, if I'm so psychic, why aren't I figuring anything out?" I murmured.

I didn't expect an answer, but Gabby gave me one, anyway.

"Practice," she said.

I don't know that I'd heard her say that word before and while she was intelligent and able to respond mostly appropriately with her catch phrases; I didn't recognize this one.

"Gabby?" I said, following a hunch. "Am I supposed to practice this psychic thing? Is that the key?"

I got chills when Gabby simply said, "Yes."

In the last twenty-four hours, I'd interacted with the police, an attorney who destroyed our equipment, an irate producer, and two ghosts multiple times and it was the parrot on my shoulder who freaked me out the most.

"Alright then," I said. "Let's practice."

I had no idea what this practice was supposed to look like, but I sure as hell wasn't going to ask the parrot any more direct questions. If she'd answered me again, I wasn't sure I could handle it.

I walked through the dimly lit corridors of Maplewood Mansion with Gabby perched on my shoulder. I tried to clear my mind and stay open to any new feelings or instincts.

As we passed by an old, ornate portrait of a man, I stopped and looked closer. A small tag told me it was Thomas Harper. I stared at it for several seconds, then started to get goosebumps up and down my arms.

I shivered involuntarily and leaned in closer. As I stared into the man's eyes, visions flooded my mind. I saw Thomas Harper and Lillian together, their expressions filled with a mix of love and desperation. Lillian cradled a baby in her arms, her face radiant with maternal affection. Then the scene shifted, and I saw Thomas digging a grave in a secluded part of the estate, his face contorted with anger and fear.

"Gabby, something's not right," I whispered, my vision blurring.

Suddenly, a wave of dizziness washed over me, and I stumbled, reaching out to steady myself against the wall. The images were overwhelming, and I could feel my heart racing. My breath came in short gasps and I tried to turn away, but my feet felt rooted to the spot, my eyes glued to the portrait.

"Jackie!" Gabby squawked, flapping her wings frantically.

The final vision was the most harrowing. I saw Lillian's lifeless body being lowered into the grave, Thomas's hands trembling as he covered her with dirt. The weight of the grief and guilt in his eyes was palpable.

Then the hallway spun, my knees turned to jello, and the ceiling lowered itself onto me, enclosing me in a dark tomb.

I woke up on the couch in the library, my head resting on a soft pillow, a blanket tucked around me. The familiar faces of my team surrounded me, their expressions filled with concern. Gabby was perched on the back of the couch, watching me intently. Ollie, who had clearly been worried, was kneeling beside me, her hand resting on my shoulder.

"Sis?" Ollie asked softly, her eyes searching mine for any sign of distress.

I blinked, trying to clear the fog from my mind. My head ached, and my body felt heavy, but I sat up with Ollie's help. The rest of the team gathered closer, their curiosity and concern evident.

"What happened?" Leo asked.

"I don't really know," I said. "I passed out. How did you find me?"

"Gabby came and got me," Ollie said. "She told me you were sick."

I smiled at Gabby. "Thanks."

Gabby flapped her wings and squawked, "Love, love, love."

"Yeah, I love you, too," I said.

"You seemed so upset when you left," Ethan said.

"We wanted to follow you, but Ollie told us no," Tyler said.

"I guess we should have," Ollie smiled regretfully. "It might have saved you from passing out. Do you need a doctor, do you think?"

"No, no. I can tell you why it happened. Give me a minute."

I asked for some water and took my time taking small sips and processing what I'd seen. Was that the vision I was looking for? Was that a psychic message telling us it was Thomas Harper who killed Lillian? It certainly appeared to be the case.

I took a deep breath, trying to steady myself. "I... I saw Thomas Harper," I began. "I saw him with Lillian and their baby. And then I saw him... burying her."

The room fell silent as my words sank in. Emily's eyes widened, and she reached out to hold my hand. "Oh, Thomas," she said. "We thought you loved her!"

I nodded, the memories of the vision still fresh and raw. "Yes, it was so clear. Thomas killed Lillian. He buried her in a shallow grave. I felt his guilt, his sorrow. He didn't want to do it, but he did."

Ethan, who had been quietly listening, spoke up. "This changes everything. If Thomas killed Lillian, it means there was a cover-up that goes back generations. Did you see the baby?"

"Yes, but not being buried. Remember, they said Lillian left to have the baby and then came back. He must have killed her when she returned," I said.

"So if the baby was never found, but Evelyn was getting close to uncovering who it is...," Emily's words trailed off.

"Then someone in the present must have wanted to stop her," Tyler finished, his expression dark. "To protect the family's reputation and whatever secrets they still have."

"And any inheritance the descendants would have a right to claim," Ethan finished.

Gabby flapped her wings. "The truth is out there!"

"Wrong genre, Gabby, but yeah, it sure is!" Leo said.

"We should start by looking through the family records and any documents we haven't reviewed yet. There might be something we've missed."

Ethan stood up, determination in his eyes. "I'll check the archives for anything related to Thomas and Lillian. There might be letters, diaries, or even legal documents that could shed more light on what happened. Now that we know to look more closely at Thomas, maybe we'll find something."

Just then, a knock on the door revealed Officer Mitchell. Emily had called the nurse emergency line at the hospital and asked for advice when I was still unconscious. They told her that as long as I didn't hit my head, it would be fine to just wake me slowly and monitor me. Apparently, they decided I'd fainted from low blood pressure or low blood sugar.

But because it was the second time in twenty-four hours that someone from this location had been injured, they notified the police.

"I saw the notification and grabbed it before anyone else did. You folks have enough to deal with as it is. So, what really happened?" Officer Mitchell asked conspiratorially.

True to form, Emily kept no secrets, especially from handsome men in uniform, and she spilled everything to him about my vision.

Once he confirmed I was okay and there was no foul play at hand, he prepared to leave.

"Hey, you know what you need?" He asked.

"What?"

"A seance. And I know just the person. Hold on. We'll be in touch."

He closed the door before I could say anything else. When I turned, everyone was looking at me with expectant expressions.

"No, absolutely not. Can you imagine if Mia got wind of that? And it's not exactly following investigative protocol. No."

With resignation, they dispersed to continue their investigation. I felt an odd sense of purpose. While the vision had been terrifying, but it had also given us a crucial piece of the puzzle.

And there was still what happened with Gabby.

I whispered, "Thanks for getting help, Gabby. You're a lifesaver."

Gabby tilted her head and squawked, "It will be okay."

I lowered my voice even more. "So, were you actually understanding and then answering my questions up there? Or was I imagining it?"

"It will be okay," she said.

CHAPTER 12

"We should do it in the library, I would think."

"We'll need to move some things around."

"And bring in that large round table, the one in the parlor."

I watched the activity from a distance. Of course I was overruled, and the seance was in full swing. Clara Mitchell was in charge and looked like she'd been born for this very moment.

"I think you need to tell her about your abilities," Ollie had whispered to me a few minutes ago. "It might be important for her to know."

I wanted to laugh at Ollie. As though anything about me would or could affect the seance, but then after what happened upstairs, I wasn't sure. Again, I felt the contradiction in myself that I could accept all these other things happening around me, but I couldn't accept that maybe I understood more than I thought, or that I had access to information others didn't have. Whatever it was, I decided to embrace it for the moment at least and tell Clara what happened upstairs. She could draw her own conclusions.

Just as I was about to talk to her, my phone rang. It was Mia.

"I assume you are packing up," she said without preamble.

"Well, no. Actually, there's been a break-through and-,"

She didn't let me finish.

"I will be there tomorrow and I will escort you off the grounds if I have to."

Then she hung up.

Clara was already watching me closely.

"You look irritated, dear," she said. "Anything I can do to help?"

"No, thank you. It's just my boss being cranky. What you're doing here, for us, this is huge. Thank you so much. Oh! And I need to tell you what happened earlier. I saw some things."

That was all it took to completely garner Clara's attention. She pulled me to a set of chairs away from everyone else and sat enthralled as I told her about my experience with the portrait and what I saw. When I finished, she shook her head slowly.

"I thought I sensed something from you. Yes, I can see it now. Like me, you don't advertise your special instincts, but others like us can usually tell. My grandson is like us too," she winked.

"I thought maybe he told you already."

"No, he didn't. There was no reason to. He knew you'd tell me."

Of course he did.

The team arranged the room carefully, following Clara's detailed instructions. The candles around the large, circular table cast eerie shadows on the walls, and the atmosphere felt charged with a strange energy. The heavy drapes were drawn shut, blocking out any remnants of daylight and leaving the room bathed in a dim, ghostly glow.

"Everyone, take your seats," Clara directed, her voice steady but low.

We all sat at our assigned places around the table. Gabby was perched on the back of my chair, unusually quiet, as if sensing the gravity of the moment.

"Alright," Clara continued. "Let's join hands and focus. We need to create a strong, unified energy to reach out to Thomas."

We clasped hands, forming a circle. I could feel the tension in the room, a mix of fear and determination. Closing my eyes, I took a deep breath, trying to steady my nerves.

Clara spoke, her voice calm and rhythmic. "Spirits of Maplewood Mansion, we call upon you. Thomas Harper, if you are here, we ask that you come forward and speak with us. We seek the truth about what happened to Lillian Moore."

For a few moments, there was only silence. The air seemed to grow colder, and I felt a chill run down my spine. Just as I wondered if anything would happen, a faint whisper echoed through the room.

"Why?"

I opened my eyes, and there, in the dim light, the ghostly figure of Thomas Harper materialized at the head of the table. His face was solemn, his eyes filled with a mix of sorrow and defiance.

Clara continued, her voice unwavering. "Thomas Harper, we know you hold the key to what happened here. We need you to tell us the truth about Lillian Moore."

Thomas's form flickered, his expression tightening. "Don't meddle. Leave."

"Thomas, we need to know the truth. What happened to Lillian?" Clara pressed him.

The ghostly figure seemed to waver. "Not my choice," he whispered, his voice filled with anguish. "Don't understand."

Clara was unrelenting. "Thomas. We need to know. Why did you kill her?"

Thomas's face twisted in anger, and his form

grew more intense, the surrounding air crackled with energy. "I did not kill Lillian!" he shouted, his voice echoing through the room. "How dare you!"

The temperature in the room dropped even further, and the candles flickered violently. The team held their breath and the atmosphere was charged with fear and tension.

Just as Thomas' anger seemed ready to erupt, a soft, ethereal glow appeared beside him. Lillian's ghost materialized, her presence calming the turbulent energy. She placed a gentle hand on Thomas's arm, her touch soothing his rage.

"Lillian," I whispered, my voice barely audible.

Lillian looked at Thomas with a tender, sorrowful expression, and then turned her gaze to us. She shook her head slowly, pointing to Thomas and then shaking her head again, clearly indicating that he was not the killer.

Thomas's form wavered, his anger dissolving into grief. "I loved her," he whispered, his voice filled with sorrow. "I could not save her."

The room grew still, the oppressive tension lifting as Lillian's calming presence spread. She looked at us with pleading eyes, urging us to understand.

Clara's voice broke the silence. "If Thomas didn't kill Lillian, then who did?"

Lillian's form shimmered, and she gestured

towards the family Bible on the table, her expression one of profound sadness.

"Secrets," Thomas said, his voice soft but clear. "Choices. A terrible price."

Lillian's form faded, and Thomas' followed. Their message was clear. Thomas was not the murderer, but the truth was still buried within the dark history of the Harper family.

As the spirits vanished, we were left in the dim light, the gravity of the revelations settling over us.

"Well," Leo said, breaking the silence, "that was intense."

Ollie nodded, her face pale but resolute. "We have our answer, but it seems there are more secrets to uncover."

I looked around at my team, feeling a mix of relief and renewed determination. "Thomas gave us a clue," I said. "We need to figure out who else was involved and what they're hiding. We have to be careful, but we can't stop now."

Clara nodded. "Agreed. Let's keep pushing forward. We're closer than ever to uncovering the truth."

We discussed having another seance, but were stuck with too many questions. What did we hope to find out this time? Who would we summon? What was the missing piece?

The air was thick with the weight of the revelations, and everyone seemed lost in their own thoughts, processing what they had experienced.

Ethan continued to flip through Evelyn's notes, muttering to himself about something he must be missing.

Emily stared at one photo after another as she chewed on her lower lip piercing.

Leo and Ollie took turns pressing rewind and play over and over on their recording devices.

Tyler stared into the middle distance, his eyes slightly crossed.

I watched the flickering flames as my mind raced. The visions, the emotions, the desperate pleas from both Thomas and Lillian–they all swirled in my head, trying to form a coherent picture. My thoughts felt like a jigsaw puzzle with too many pieces missing.

Gabby, now perched quietly on my shoulder, occasionally muttered, "Same truth," her voice soft but insistent.

Suddenly, it all clicked into place. Gabby was right. It was the same truth! I jumped up, startling everyone around me.

"Same truth! Evelyn and Lillian appeared to me together when they told me the killer wasn't Bob or Phillip. But whose killer? Whose killer wasn't Bob or Phillip? They know we are looking for who murdered them both, so why would they both appear to steer us in a different direction?"

Everyone looked at me. Some had expressions of concern, no doubt wondering if I had indeed struck my head when I passed out. Others looked curious. Only one of them was smiling.

"They were both killed by the same person," Clara said.

"Exactly!" I pointed at Clara.

Ollie looked up, her face one of the concerned ones. "But Jackie, there's over a century between their deaths. How could the same person be responsible?"

I looked at Clara for encouragement. "Go on, dear," she said. "You know how."

I paced the room, my mind racing as I tried to put my thoughts into words. "It's not about the same person in a physical sense. It's the same entity, the same malevolent force that has been haunting this place."

Leo began rubbing his temples again and asked, "Are you suggesting a ghost killed them both?"

I nodded, the realization sinking in. "Yes. Think about it. Lillian was the cause of the mansion's darkest secret, and Evelyn was close to uncovering it. They were both silenced to keep those secrets buried."

Emily leaned forward, her eyes wide with intrigue. "But how can a ghost kill someone? And why would it care about these secrets?"

"The spirits here are not just trapped echoes of the past," I explained, my voice gaining confidence. "They interact with the living. They protect the secrets that they were part of, even in death. The Harper family had many secrets, and those who threatened to expose them were silenced."

Ollie looked thoughtful, trying to piece together the implications. "So, if Evelyn was killed by a ghost, then it means the spirit is acting out of a sense of duty to protect those secrets."

"A sense of duty, a sense of pride, a sense of honor..."

I nodded, my heart pounding with the gravity of what I was saying. "Exactly. And that spirit could have been someone who was part of those secrets. Someone who would do anything to keep them hidden."

I stopped pacing and looked at my team, feeling a mixture of fear and determination. "Evelyn was killed by a ghost," I said firmly. "And that means we're dealing with a powerful, malevolent force that will stop at nothing to protect the dark history of Maplewood Mansion."

"But who then, if not Thomas? Especially since you saw Thomas in your vision burying Lillian?" Ollie asked.

The room fell silent. The flickering candlelight seemed to cast deeper shadows, and the air grew colder.

"I don't know. Maybe my vision was wrong. But that doesn't change the fact that we need to follow this to the end."

"We're going to need another seance," Clara whispered as she clapped her hands.

~

"We need to call Lillian and Thomas again and ask who killed Lillian."

"And call Evelyn. Ask who killed her."

"It's not like we haven't been asking those questions, though!"

"Right! That's our entire purpose for being here. If it was as simple as just asking them, we'd already have an answer."

"Exactly! All they tell us is who it isn't. Or that we're looking in the wrong place. And I still don't know what that was supposed to mean," I added my comment to the others.

We were setting up the room again for our second seance. Everyone running to the bathroom, getting water, stretching...and offering ideas that weren't very helpful.

"Maybe they are afraid to say it," Clara suggested. "If there is a malevolent spirit here, it isn't one of those three. So, who would try to keep them quiet? That's what we need to find out."

Everyone stopped rushing around when she said this. The stakes had just increased tenfold. We were about to challenge a malevolent spirit who, if we were correct, had killed two people, one of whom was murdered in modern times right where we were sitting.

"Alright," Clara began. "Like last time, join hands and focus. We need to create a strong, unified energy to reach out to Evelyn, Lillian, and Thomas."

We clasped hands, forming a circle once more. I closed my eyes and took a deep breath, feeling the weight of the moment settle over me.

Clara spoke, her voice calm and rhythmic. "Spirits of Maplewood Mansion, we call upon you. Evelyn Carter, Lillian Moore, and Thomas Harper, we ask that you come forward and speak with us. We seek the truth about what happened to Lillian."

For a few moments, there was only silence. The air grew colder, and I felt a familiar chill run down my spine. Just as I wondered if they would answer us again, the faint outlines of three ghostly figures materialized before us.

Evelyn, Lillian, and Thomas stood together, their forms shimmering in the candlelight.

"Evelyn, Lillian, Thomas," Clara said, her voice

strong and sure. "It is time for you to be brave and tell us, who killed Lillian? Who killed Evelyn?"

Thomas's face twisted with anguish, and he looked at Lillian, his eyes filled with regret. "Not me," he said, his voice filled with sorrow. "I loved her."

Evelyn stepped forward, her form flickering. "The truth is hidden," she whispered. "Look deeper."

"OMG," Ollie muttered under her breath.

"No more games," Clara's voice thundered. "A name. Who?"

The air grew colder, and the flickering candles dimmed. It was hard to breathe, and I shivered involuntarily.

Thomas stepped forward. He looked around, then at Lillian. With frightened eyes still darting around, he said, "Mother."

Then the three ghosts disappeared.

The temperature in the room dropped sharply. The flickering candles went out at once, plunging us into darkness. Then a cold, howling wind swept through the room, and the air grew thick with an oppressive energy.

A terrible, loud rumble echoed through the mansion, shaking the very walls. The ground beneath us trembled, and I could hear the distant sound of objects crashing to the floor.

"What's happening?" Emily shouted over the din, her voice filled with fear.

The wind intensified, whipping around us as if trying to force us out of the room. The cold was bone-chilling, and the darkness seemed to press in from all sides.

Everyone was standing by now, unsure of what to do.

"Stay together!" Clara yelled, her voice barely audible over the cacophony. "Keep holding hands. We need to end the séance and get out of here!"

And then, just as suddenly as it had begun, the wind ceased, and the room fell into an eerie silence. The only sound was our heavy breathing.

I clutched the table, my heart pounding in my chest. "You're right. We need to get out of here," I whispered, my voice barely more than a breath.

We gathered our things as quickly as possible. And we ran.

CHAPTER 13

W e were in the hallway on our way to the front door when the temperature plummeted yet again. The air grew thick with an intense, almost suffocating cold. We stopped in our tracks, the hairs on the back of our necks standing up. A chilling wind whipped through the hallway, our flashlights went out and we were plunged into darkness.

"Everyone, stay close," Ollie whispered, her voice filled with tension. "Let's keep going."

Before we could take another step, a ghostly figure materialized in front of us. It was an angry, terrifying spirit. Her eyes blazed with fury, and her presence filled the hallway with a menacing energy.

"Here's Johnny," Gabby said. Her talons

gripped my shoulder and she flapped her wings nervously.

"Who is asking questions? Why was I awoken?" she demanded, her voice echoing through the dark corridor.

We stood frozen, the intensity of her anger almost tangible.

I stepped forward, my heart pounding in my chest. "We are looking for the truth." I said, trying to keep my voice steady.

The ghost's eyes narrowed, and her form flickered violently. "You have no right to meddle in my affairs," she hissed. "My story is of no importance to you."

"Yes, it is. We need to understand what happened to Lillian and Evelyn. We need to find justice for them."

"Justice?" the ghost spat, her voice dripping with disdain. "There is no justice here, only the protection of my family's legacy. You are meddling in matters you do not understand."

"Just tell us why," I said. "Why did you kill Lillian?"

I took a chance assuming this malevolent being was Lillian's killer. It wasn't a terribly hard guess, but it was awfully hard to say it.

The ghost's eyes blazed with an otherworldly light, and she floated closer, her presence almost overwhelming. To my surprise, she readily admitted it.

"I did what I had to do to protect my family. Lillian was a threat. So was Evelyn. They would have brought ruin upon us all. I did what was necessary. The Harper legacy had to be preserved, no matter the cost. And now you are here, threatening it again. Leave now."

Clara squared her shoulders and faced the ghost. By way of an answer, the rest of us did the same. We were a small and terrified group, but we stood shoulder to shoulder in the name of justice.

"Then you will face my wrath," she screamed with a deafening roar. Then she lunged toward us, her form a terrifying blur of rage and power. The wind howled, and the darkness seemed to close in around us, suffocating and relentless.

"Everyone, run!" Ollie shouted.

Since she blocked the door, we turned around and ran back towards the library as the ghost's enraged screams echoed behind us. The oppressive cold followed us. We tripped over our own feet, numb from the cold. We raced through the mansion, our hearts pounding.

As we ran back down the hallway, our footsteps echoed through the dark and cold mansion. Her oppressive presence followed us, her furious energy growing stronger. We barely made it back to the library when her ghostly form materialized before us, once again blocking our path. Her eyes blazed with an unearthly light, her fury palpable.

"You dare speak of justice?" she screamed, her voice reverberating off the walls. "What do you know of justice? What about justice for me?"

We halted, breathless and terrified, as her spectral form advanced. Her presence was overwhelming, a cold wind swirling around her, making the candles flicker wildly.

"Who are you to judge me?" she continued, her voice dripping with venom. "You come here accusing me of crimes, but you know nothing of the sacrifices I made, the pain I endured! Do you know what it feels like to be betrayed by your own blood?"

Her ghostly form flickered, the rage in her eyes momentarily giving way to a deep, haunting sorrow. "I was killed by my own kin. Murdered by the son I raised, the boy I loved. My baby, my Thomas."

The room grew even colder as the wind howled through the mansion, amplifying the ghost's torment.

The chilling revelation hung in the air as the weight of her words sank in. We barely had a moment to process what we had just learned when the oppressive cold intensified again.

"You dare uncover my secrets?" she screamed, her voice a terrifying wail. "You will pay for your insolence!"

Before we could react, objects around the room lifted off the ground, floating ominously. Books, candlesticks, the fire poker, and other items were yanked from their places and hurled through the air. We ducked and scrambled to avoid the projectiles, the fear in the room was palpable.

"Get down!" Leo shouted, pulling Emily to the floor just as a heavy book flew past their heads.

Ollie tried to shield herself behind a chair, but it was quickly ripped away and tossed aside by an unseen force. "She's too powerful!" she yelled, her voice filled with panic.

I felt a sharp pain as a candlestick struck my shoulder, knocking me off balance. Gabby squawked in alarm, fluttering to a safer perch out of reach of the flying objects.

"We need to get out of here!" I shouted, trying to gather my wits. "Everyone, head for the French doors!"

The ghost's laughter echoed through the room, cold and cruel. "You think you can escape me? You cannot outrun the past!"

More objects flew at us, smashing into walls and

shattering on the floor. A vase narrowly missed Ollie, crashing into the wall beside her. Tyler shielded his head with his arms as debris rained down around us.

"Move, move!" Ethan urged, helping Emily to her feet and pushing her towards the French doors.

We bolted for the exit, dodging the ghost's relentless assault. The doors seemed so far away, the path to it littered with obstacles. I felt the ghost's fury pressing down on us, her energy crackling through the air.

As we neared the doorway, a heavy bookcase toppled over, aimed directly at us. "Watch out!" Leo shouted, grabbing my arm and pulling me out of the way just in time.

We stumbled through the door, the ghost's enraged screams following us. The moment we crossed the threshold, the icy wind stopped, and the door slammed shut behind us.

"Keep going!" I urged, my voice hoarse with fear. "Get further away from the house." The clear night air was a stark contrast to the oppressive atmosphere inside the mansion. We huddled together on the lawn, trembling from the ordeal.

"Is everyone okay?" I asked in a shaky voice.

Emily nodded, still clutching Ethan's arm for support. "I think so. But that was... she was so angry."

"She won't stop," Ollie said, her voice filled with

dread. "She won't let us go until we leave this place or we finish what we started."

Leo rubbed his shoulder where a flying object had hit him. "We can't go back in there, not like this. We need a plan."

I looked back at the mansion, the dark windows stared at us like eyes filled with malevolence. "We need to find a way to deal with her. To put her spirit to rest."

Together, we stood in the cold night while the mansion loomed before us.

Looking up at the mansion, we saw two ghostly figures standing in the window of the grand parlor. Lillian and Evelyn, their ethereal forms glowed softly in the darkness.

"Look!" Emily whispered, pointing up.

We all turned our gaze upwards, watching the two spirits as they seemed to reach out to us, their expressions filled with a mix of sorrow and urgency. But before we could react, a dark shadow crept over them, swallowing their light.

"No!" Ollie gasped, clutching my arm.

The shadow overtook the window, and the entire mansion seemed to shudder, as if it was alive and reacting to the malevolent presence within.

Gabby flapped her wings nervously, squawking, "Redrum! Redrum!"

I looked around at my team, seeing the fear in their eyes.

"What do we do?" I asked.

"That was Thomas's mother?" Tyler said. "And Thomas killed her?" His voice was incredulous.

"Was that the body you saw him burying in your vision?" Ollie asked. "Not Lillian, but his mother?"

I nodded. "Must be. I can't believe this."

"We have to save them," Emily said. "She's keeping them here."

Leo nodded, still rubbing his shoulder. "But how? We can't go back in there."

Clara, who had been deep in thought, finally spoke up. "There must be a way to break her hold on the mansion. Spirits like hers are bound by unfinished business or strong emotional ties. Sometimes it's their remains, or a significant memento they refuse to leave behind. If we can find out what's keeping her here, we can potentially release her."

Ollie nodded in agreement. "And we have to protect ourselves. We can't face her unprepared."

I took a deep breath, feeling a renewed sense of purpose. "Okay. What do we know about Thomas's mother and her connection to the mansion? There has to be something we've overlooked, something that can help us."

"We don't have any information with us. Everything is still inside," Ethan said.

"No, wait!" Leo said, pulling his phone from his pocket. "I took pictures and video of lots of the research. You guys wouldn't let me do anything, so I snuck all this stuff, so I could keep working. Look, here is the family tree."

He handed his phone to Ollie, who snatched it away from him. As she studied the photo, she mumbled, "Little stinker, not supposed to be on monitors and using this thing."

But when she found the name, she whispered it. "Julia. Her name is Julia."

"Clara, what do you know about Julia Harper? Ethan? Anything?" I asked.

"Not off the top of my head, but let me see that," Ethan said. Ollie handed him the smart phone, and he looked at it, then turned it over. The screen went black, and he shook it once.

"Do this," Clara said as she poked the phone with her pointer finger.

"Here, give it to me," Emily said. "Old people, and Leo, follow me."

Emily, Ethan, Leo, and Clara sat on the low wall surrounding the mansion and began going through the information Leo had tucked away on his smartphone.

CHAPTER 14

It was cold outside, not as cold as inside, but still. Thankfully, there was some gear in the van and we pulled out extra blankets, sweatshirts, and sweaters to keep warm. The team had separated into small groups, heads bent together, trying to make sense of what we'd learned.

I found myself drifting away again, lost in thought. Being outside and being alone brought back those strange feelings. Something was nagging at the back of my mind.

I walked a little distance away from the camp and sat down on an old, weathered bench, the chill seeping through my pants making my butt colder than it already was. Gabby fluttered over and perched on my shoulder.

I pulled her onto my lap and wrapped my arms around her.

As I stared at the dark silhouette of Maple-wood Mansion, as usual, the stress caused memories of my sister Sophie to flood my mind.

"Not now," I said to myself. "I need to focus."

I closed my eyes, but instead of focusing on the current situation, the memories kept distracting me. Grandma had always believed in my intuition, in the strange ability I had to see things others couldn't. The same intuition that had led me to Sophie's grave, but no further in solving her murder.

The image in my mind of that shallow grave appeared sharp, but then it grew fuzzy along the edges. I blinked, trying to focus my mind's eye. As Sophie's grave faded away, another replaced it. It was the same grave from my vision. When I'd seen Thomas burying who I thought was Lillian, but was actually his mother.

Taking a deep breath, I focused inward, letting the noise of the camp and the chill of the night fade away. I concentrated on the visions I saw, the emotions they stirred, and the energy that guided me before.

"Show me," I whispered.

Gabby, sensing my concentration, remained quiet, her presence grounding me. I felt a strange warmth spread through my body, a tingling sensation that grew stronger as I focused on Julia and her connection to the mansion.

Images formed in my mind, faint and flickering at first, but growing clearer with each passing moment. I saw the mansion as it had been a century ago, its grounds well-tended and vibrant. I saw Thomas, a young man filled with grief and rage, digging a grave under the cover of darkness.

The scene shifted, and I followed him as he carried a lifeless body wrapped in a shroud. I could feel his sorrow, his guilt, and his determination to hide the terrible truth. He carried that body deep in the woods, away from prying eyes, and laid it near a small tree.

I gasped as the vision faded as quickly as it had come. My heart pounded in my chest, and I felt a mixture of fear and determination.

"We need her bones," I whispered, more to myself than to Gabby. "And I know where they are."

The cool night air bit into my skin as I ran towards the backyard of Maplewood Mansion, my breath coming in quick bursts. The vision of Thomas Harper burying his mother's body beneath the Japanese Maple was burned into my mind, guiding my steps through the dark, overgrown garden.

"Gabby, go get the others," I urged, my voice trembling with urgency. "We need everyone here."

145

Gabby squawked in response and took off into the night, her wings flapping silently as she soared back to the camp. I continued running, the eerie silence of the night amplifying my footsteps on the frozen ground.

"It will look different now," I told myself. "The tree will be bigger."

I stopped and scanned the woods. There. That had to be it. The tree was bigger, but Japanese Maples grow slowly. Its unique shape standing out among the other trees in the woods.

I dropped to the ground and sat cross-legged while I waited. Within moments, I heard the sounds of hurried footsteps and the worried calls of my team. Gabby was leading them through the garden, her squawks guiding them towards me.

"Jackie, what's going on?" Ollie asked, breathless, as she reached my side.

"I saw it," I said, my voice shaking. "I saw where Thomas buried his mother. It's right here, under this tree."

Emily looked at me with wide eyes. "Are you sure?"

I nodded, the urgency of the vision still coursing through me. "We need to dig. We need to find her bones."

Tyler and Leo exchanged a glance before nodding. "Let's get to it, then," Tyler said.

We spread out, searching for anything we

could use as a shovel. Leo found an old gardening shed nearby, and we quickly gathered shovels and other tools. The cold metal felt heavy in my hands, but I knew we had to act fast.

The ground was hard and unyielding, the cold making it difficult to break through the surface. Thankfully, Japanese Maples also have small root systems so we didn't have to wrestle our way through thick, heavy roots like on the ones nearby.

Tyler, Ethan, Emily and Leo worked together, their shovels biting into the earth with a determined rhythm.

As they dug, the wind picked up, rustling the branches of the maple. The night seemed to close in around us, the oppressive presence of Julia Harper's ghost was palpable.

Finally, the shovels broke through to softer ground and in the light of the moon, we saw something yellowish glinting in the hole.

We carefully brushed away as much of the soil as possible without disturbing the remains. With an uneasy glance at the team, I reached in and picked up what I thought was an arm. It felt rough but gave way with the lightest touch.

"What do we need to do with them?" I asked Clara.

"We should show Julia that we have them and that her hold over the house has been broken. We need to bury them somewhere other than here, too. A proper burial."

I attempted to lift another of the bones and felt it give under my gentle touch. "This will take forever," I said. "Do we have to remove them all?"

Clara shook her head. "No, not all of them. Just enough so she knows it is hers. Can you get her skull?"

I felt my stomach flip and tasted vomit in the back of my throat. Was I really trying to pluck this woman's skull from the shallow grave her son had put her in? I did not sign up for this.

"Here, let me," Tyler said, nudging me to the side.

I paused. This would be the worst possible time for Tyler to have a clumsy accident. He noticed my hesitation.

"Trust me," he said. "I've got this."

I nodded and moved out of his way. He reached into the grave. His large hands cradled the skull gently while keeping it together and intact. He turned towards Ollie who was holding out a sweatshirt and they quickly bundled it up.

"Okay, gang," Clara said. "Back to it!"

I know I hesitated, and I got the sense the rest of the team did as well. None of us was eager to meet Julia again, much less now that we had her head wrapped in a University of Tennessee orange sweatshirt.

"Do you want me to do it, dear?" Clara asked. "I've had a bit more experience and ...,"

I stopped her from saying anything more.

"No, I'll do it. It's my job."

We moved quickly back toward Maplewood Mansion. The night seemed darker and colder, the oppressive presence of Julia seemed to grow stronger with each step. The mansion loomed ahead, its dark windows watching us like eyes.

We entered the house. I led with Clara and the rest of the team right on my heels.

"What do I do?" I asked.

"We'll have to face her. We have to show her what we've found," Clara answered.

"Where is -," I started to ask, but Julia appeared before I finished my question. Her eyes blazing with fury. Her presence filled the room with that same oppressive coldness that made it hard to breathe.

"How dare you return!" she screeched, her voice echoing through the room. "You will pay for your insolence!"

The wind howled louder, and objects around the room began to shake and lift off the ground. The oppressive energy pressed down on us, but we stood our ground.

"These are your bones!" I shouted, holding up

the orange and white sweatshirt. "We found where Thomas buried you, and we have your skull."

The ghost's eyes widened with a mix of rage and terror. "No! You cannot do this! Put it down and leave!"

With those words, I knew exactly what I needed to do next. She wanted me to leave her bones here, which meant I absolutely had to take them away.

"No," I said. "Your spirit has haunted this place long enough. It's time for you to leave."

Julia screamed, a sound filled with pain and fury, causing the very walls of the mansion to tremble. The force of her rage sent objects flying, and the wind grew stronger, nearly knocking us off our feet.

With the sweatshirt-wrapped bones clutched tightly in my hands, I knew what I had to do. I had to get her remains out of the house and off the property.

"We need to get these bones out of here," I said, my voice steady despite the fear gnawing at me. "Let's go."

The team nodded in agreement, but as I turned to leave, Julia moved faster. She appeared in front of me, once again blocking my path.

"You will not take my remains!" she screamed, her voice echoing with a terrifying intensity. "I will not let you destroy me!"

The wind howled. I tightened my grip on the bones, tucked my head down and ran. I was determined to get out of the mansion no matter what. The others followed close behind, trying to shield themselves from the ghost's relentless assault while at the same time helping me escape.

As I sprinted through the darkened hallways, the ghost's presence pressed down on me, making it harder to breathe. The air grew colder with each step, and I could feel her malevolent energy closing in.

"You cannot escape me!" she shrieked, her voice filled with rage.

Just when I thought I couldn't go any further, a soft, ethereal glow appeared in front of me. The ghostly forms of Lillian, Evelyn, and Thomas materialized."

"Go!" Lillian urged, her voice echoing through the hall.

Evelyn and Thomas stepped forward, their ghostly hands reaching out to hold back the malevolent spirit. The surrounding air crackled with energy as they formed a barrier, giving me a chance to escape.

"Hurry," Thomas said, his voice strained.

I nodded, feeling a surge of gratitude. "Thank you," I whispered. "I won't let you down."

With renewed energy, I continued to run, the ghostly figures of Lillian, Evelyn, and Thomas fading behind me as they struggled to contain the furious spirit.

I heard my team cheering me on and I kept my head down, my focus on the door and the path to freedom. The ethereal barrier held just long enough for me to reach the front door. I pushed it open with all my strength and stumbled through.

Almost immediately, the weight lifted, but I didn't stop. With Julia's bones still clutched tightly in my arms, I started down the road.

CHAPTER 15

By the time I reached the end of the drive, I was shivering uncontrollably. Partly from fear, partly from relief, but mostly from the cold. I briefly wondered how awful it would be if I put on the sweatshirt I was carrying.

Thankfully, I didn't have to make that decision. A car was approaching quickly, and I held up a hand. It screeched to a stop inches away from me and of all the people it could have been, Mia jumped out.

"Jackie! What the hell are you doing out here at the crack of dawn? You better be leaving. Where is everyone else? What are you carrying?"

I gaped at her, uncertain which question to answer first.

"Mia, thank goodness! I'm freezing."

"Get in," she ordered.

I gratefully sat in her front seat, keeping my macabre package in my lap, and reveled in the heat.

"Now talk," she said.

"We did it. We found out who is haunting the mansion, and we solved Evelyn's murder. Plus, there's an entire backstory that will be great for the show."

Mia held up a hand. "Stop right there. I don't want to hear your ghost stories. I told the execs what was going on here and they are pulling the show. There will not be a 'Haunted Mysteries.' Like I've said a million times, you and your team need to pack up and leave. In fact, good for you! It looks like you are already doing that."

She nodded towards the shirt with the skull wrapped inside.

"Tell you what, I'll drive you back up to the house and you can gather up the rest of your crew. Load up into the van and drive away. No more running around out here in the middle of the road."

"No!" I said, "Mia, we can't go back there! You don't understand."

I kept talking, trying to explain, but she spoke over me, louder and more insistent. Finally, I just stopped talking, and she finished by saying, "You're fired."

"You are a terrible producer, Mia," I said.

She shook her head slowly. "You know, Jackie. I've tried to help you. You and your weird ideas and your weird friends. And that gawd awful bird of yours. I'm done. Just get out. Consider yourself fired. I'll let you tell the team."

"Fine," I said as I climbed from the car. I barely had the door closed before Mia was gunning the engine. She peeled away from me with tires spinning.

As I walked back towards the mansion, the adrenaline from my encounter with Mia slowly faded, leaving me feeling both exhausted and exhilarated. The morning was still cold, and my breath puffed in front of me in the crisp air. I could see the mansion in the distance and it already looked lighter somehow.

Then I saw the silhouettes of Ollie and Gabby coming towards me. Gabby flapped her wings and squawked loudly, clearly relieved to see me.

"Jackie!" Ollie called out, her voice tinged with concern. "We were worried. What happened?"

I hurried towards them, a smile breaking out on my face despite everything. "You'll never believe what just happened."

Gabby perched on my shoulder, tilted her head as if urging me to spill the details. "Tell the truth!"

Ollie raised an eyebrow. "Where is the skull?"

I took a deep breath, still catching my breath from the run. "I ran into Mia. She was coming up the street, and she was furious. Started yelling at me about how we should be gone by now and how we're all fired."

Ollie frowned. "Great. Just what we need right now."

I shook my head, a grin spreading across my face. "But get this. She was so busy yelling at me, she didn't notice that I left her a little something."

Ollie's eyes widened in surprise, and then she burst out laughing. "You did what?"

"I figured it was the quickest way to get Julia's bones as far away from the house as possible," I explained, chuckling along with her. "Mia was so caught up in her rant, she didn't even see me do it."

Ollie wiped a tear from her eye, still laughing. "Jackie, you're a genius. I can just imagine Mia driving around with a skull in her car. Serves her right for being such a pain."

I laughed too, the tension of the night easing just a bit. "I thought it was the best way to keep them safe and buy us some time. Now we just need to figure out our next steps for here."

Ollie nodded, her laughter fading into a more serious expression. "We still need to put Julia's spirit to rest. But at least we have the bones out of the mansion and can focus on the others first."

I nodded in agreement, feeling a renewed sense of determination. "How is it in there now?"

"As soon as you were out of the house, Julia's

ghost lost her power. Then I guess the further away her bones were, the easier it was for Lillian, Thomas and Evelyn to subdue her. She finally disappeared, probably because of Mia, but I don't know that she's really gone, you know?"

I nodded, feeling a mix of relief and uncertainty. "Yeah, and honestly, even if Julia's spirit is truly gone, we aren't finished. We still have to deal with Lillian, Evelyn, Thomas, and any other spirits who might be tied to this place. We can't leave until we know they're all at peace."

Ollie sighed, running a hand through her hair. "This mansion has so many layers of history, Jackie. It's like peeling back an onion. Every time we think we've reached the core, we find another layer."

We reached the front door of the mansion, and I paused, my hand resting on the doorknob. The cold metal sent a shiver down my spine, and I hesitated for a moment.

"Ready?" I asked.

Ollie nodded, and we both took a deep breath before pushing the door open. The mansion's interior was eerily silent, the air still and cold. The atmosphere seemed less intense, but it was still there, a reminder of the spirits that lingered.

We stepped inside; the floorboards creaking under our weight. The flickering candlelight from our earlier séance cast long shadows on the walls, and I felt a chill run down my spine.

"Last I saw, everyone was in the library," Ollie said.

$$\approx$$

"Hello?" I called out as Ollie, Gabby and I entered the room. After all we'd been through, I didn't want to startle anyone.

Everyone turned towards us with smiles, but Emily and Ethan were pale, Leo was pacing and Clara was sitting down with a cup of tea Tyler had apparently made for her.

"What?" I asked. "What's wrong?"

"Oh, Jackie," Emily said. "Thank goodness you are okay."

"Yeah, I'm fine. I have a funny story, but first... what's going on? You all look like you've seen a ghost."

Tyler snort laughed, and I had to smile. I hadn't realized what I'd said, but it was sort of funny.

Everyone else smiled as well, but no one else had the energy to laugh.

"We've found some things," Leo began, his voice somber.

"Lillian showed us where to find them," Tyler added.

"Once Thomas's mother was gone, Lillian and Evelyn had more power. They could help us and..."

"Guys! What?"

Ethan sighed. "It turns out that the vision you saw was real. The vision of Thomas burying a body. It was him burying his mother."

"Right, we know that."

"Because his mother killed Lillian," Ethan finished. "Thomas killed her out of revenge for Lillian."

"Oh, my," I covered my mouth. This was a terrible story. So tragic and sad. I sat down with a thump and held my head in my hands.

"You guys, there has to be something good from all of this. We still don't know who killed Evelyn - although maybe it was Julia - and we don't know if Lillian's baby survived. All this work and we really haven't solved anything."

Everyone grew quiet as the implications became more apparent.

"Oh," I added. "And we're all fired."

CHAPTER 16

"I can't believe we're just leaving," Ollie said as she slung her bag into the back of the van.

"I know. I agree. But I don't know what else to do. We're fired. I can't pay anyone for their time and I'm afraid if we don't leave now, Mia will send someone to take the van and then we're all going to be stranded here."

"Still. I'll bet everyone would stay, you know, just to see it finished."

"Ollie, I can't ask them to do that. In fact, I have to tell them the opposite. It would destroy careers if it got out that even after being fired and working on a spectacularly failed project, everyone stayed on and worked for free. Who's going to hire them then? And the network might actually keep you and Leo, especially if you just do what they want," I explained.

"Hello! Hello! Are you leaving already?"

Clara had gone home after her tea last night and although it had only been a few hours, she was back again.

"Yes, we have to go," I said. "The network fired us all, and it seems we've hit a dead end with the investigation, so it's likely just as well."

"Oh, dear," Clara fussed. "Well, I have something I must show you. After I left, I kept thinking about a strange photograph I remember my grandmother showing me. She swore to me that there was a ghost in the photo and I always thought she was teasing me. You know, she knew about my gift as well, but this was before I fully accepted it. You know, like you are now, dear."

Ollie let out a snort and covered her laugh with the back of her hand. I cleared my throat and glared at her.

"Okay, Clara. Thank you for that. What do you want to show me?"

"This."

Clara thrust an old black-and-white photo into my hands. In the light of the morning sun, it was hard to make out the details, but I could see what remained of today's Harper family. There was Margaret, whose journals helped us get started with the investigation. Next to her was her brother, Edward. And then Edward's children.

"See, right here," Clara pointed. "You have

Robert, Anne and Philip. And look, right here, behind Philip."

"No way," Ollie said.

Clara smiled and one eyebrow shot up. "Still want to call it quits?"

"No," I said. "No, I do not."

We gathered in the library one more time and passed the photo around. Everyone stared, then expressed surprise and shock. And no small amount of disbelief.

I struggled to believe as well, yet there it was, in grainy black and white, then enhanced by Ollie's technical brilliance. The Harper family as they were just a few years ago. The remaining children of Charles Harper, Thomas's older brother, Margaret and Edward. And then Edward's children Robert, Anne and Philip. But standing behind Philip was another figure. One we might not have recognized were it not for the time we'd spent in the mansion. Standing behind Philip, with one hand resting possessively on his shoulder, was Julia Harper's ghost.

"What does this mean?" Asked Emily.

"Do you think Philip knew about Julia?" Ethan asked.

My mind wandered back to my conversation

with him when he first hired us. "I don't know if he knew about Julia, but when he hired us for this and said we could film here, he commented that we needed to either debunk the haunted house theory, or, and I'm quoting him here, 'get rid of her.' I thought he meant Evelyn's ghost, but could he have been talking about Julia?"

"There is evidence of the mansion having been haunted long before Evelyn perished here," Clara said. "And it's always been malevolent. I know those stories aren't about dear Lillian or Evelyn." Clara sighed. "Oh, and here is another photo for you, Jackie." She reached into her pocked and pulled out a more modern photo of Evelyn. "I thought you might like this as a memento."

"Yes, thank you," I said. I stared at the photo and as I did, the edges grew wavy. I heard a voice as clear as day say, "Please figure it out. I'm not strong enough. You have to do it."

My head snapped up, and I looked around. "Did you guys hear that?"

"What?"

"Heard nothing."

"Nope."

I looked to my left and right and listened intently again. "Someone spoke to me," I said.

"What did they say?" Ollie asked.

"Please figure it out. I'm not strong enough. You have to do it." I repeated.

"And you heard it while looking at the photo of Evelyn," Clara piped up. "Tells me she's trying to communicate with you." She dragged out the 'u' on the last word in a singsong voice as she wiggled her finger at me.

She was way too happy about this situation.

"Fine," I groused. "I'll try this psychic stuff. It never really works though when I try too hard. And if it's important to me, well, it definitely doesn't work. It's like my emotional attachment ruins it all."

I sat down at the seance table and looked at the photo. I tried to relax and let images come to me, but I saw nothing. I closed my eyes tight and clenched my hands into fists, but still nothing.

Then I heard chairs moving and feet shuffling. I opened my eyes to see my team, Tyler, Ethan, Emily, Leo, Ollie, and even Clara, sitting at the table with me. All with their eyes closed and holding hands. I reached out and took Ollie and Tyler's hands and squeezed them both. They returned the squeeze, and I relaxed.

Within seconds, I saw Evelyn. A young woman, hair in a ponytail with a notebook under her arm. She was knocking on a door. It was answered by Philip Harper.

I had a terrible feeling about what I was seeing, but was helpless. I saw her show him her notebook. She was smiling, tears welled up in her eyes.

Philip looked uneasy, but eventually, he hugged her and smiled as well.

Evelyn left that house and returned to the mansion. I saw her sitting right where we were at that moment. She sat at a desk.

I opened my eyes and saw her ghost as clearly as if she were real. She looked up from her notebook and smiled at me. I smiled back. Then I saw Julia. She swooped around Evelyn, watching her, trying to harm her, but she couldn't. Evelyn pulled her sweater tighter around her neck and continued her reading.

A tap on the library door. Evelyn looked up and smiled. It was Philip. She called him Uncle Philip and ran to hug him. To my horror, Julia swooped in again and settled on Philip's shoulder. She was whispering to him and pointing at Evelyn. Before I could scream, "Watch out!" Philip had taken the fire poker and swung it towards Evelyn's head.

I saw Evelyn's spirit leave her body. She looked at me and said, "Thank you."

"I'm calling Tiny," Clara said.

"Who's Tiny?" Ollie asked.

"My grandson, of course."

Within a few minutes, Officer Mitchell, now

and forever to be known as Officer Tiny, pulled up to the entrance of the mansion. Clara quickly filled him in on what we had discovered, while cautioning him about what to reveal to Detective Ryan and the rest of the squad.

"I know, Grams. I know what to say and what not to say."

He took our statements, the ones we would tell him and the ones we would tell the rest of the world.

"We have that fire poker still in evidence," he said. "We just never worried about testing it for Philip. Of course, it will have his fingerprints on it, but there was blood other than Evelyn's. My bet is, it'll be his."

We walked to his patrol car as he promised to let us know the results of the test.

"We're picking up Philip right now," he added. "Get in Grams, I'll drive you home."

"Can I run the siren?" She asked with a mischievous grin.

"Of course you can."

Clara waved goodbye as they pulled away and we heard a single 'woooooo' as the lights on the car flashed once.

"Well, you did it," Ollie said, smiling at me.

"We did it," I corrected her. "Unfortunately, this was our one and only show."

The team gathered round. "It was great

working with you guys," I said. "I'm really sorry it didn't work out better. And I will do my very best to help you find other jobs."

"I think I'm finished," Ethan said. "This was the most fun I've had in a long time and if I can't do this with you all, then I don't want to work. I'll just enjoy my retirement and let this one keep me in the loop," he nodded towards Emily.

"I'm going to go back to school and finish my degree," she said.

"Leo, Tyler, I'll put in a good word for both of you at the network if you want."

"Thank you, Jackie," Tyler said. "That means a lot."

Leo nodded. "Yeah, thanks. That would be great. Ollie, will you stay at the network too?"

"Nah," Ollie said. "Any place too stupid to keep Jackie around doesn't deserve me working for them."

"I admire your modesty," I said, hugging Ollie.

"Okay, gang, let's load up and get out of here!"

Gabby flew to my shoulder and as we pulled away from Maplewood Mansion, she said, "We came, we saw, we kicked it's a-,"

"Gabby!"

CHAPTER 17

Tyler Reed: Take 4

"Welcome back to the conclusion of 'Murder at Maplewood Mansion.' Over the past few days, we've uncovered a web of secrets that have haunted this historic estate for generations.

We discovered that the mansion was once home to Lillian Moore and Thomas Harper, two individuals whose tragic love story set the stage for the hauntings that plagued this house. Lillian's untimely death at the hands of Thomas's mother Julia Harper, driven by a desire to protect the family's reputation, left a dark stain on the mansion's history.

But that wasn't the end of the story. Consumed by grief and rage, Thomas took his mother's life, burying her body and attempting to hide the truth. This cycle of tragedy continued to haunt the Harper family, eventually drawing Lillian and Thomas's great-granddaughter back to the mansion.

Yes, Evelyn Carter, unaware of her true heritage, sought to uncover the secrets of her family's past, but her quest led to her own untimely death. Her spirit, along with those of Lillian and Thomas, remained bound to the mansion, seeking closure and justice.

And justice was indeed found. Philip Harper has been arrested for the murder of Evelyn Carter."

Tyler pauses and looked intently into the camera.

"Through our investigation, we were able to uncover the truth, bringing peace to the spirits of Lillian, Thomas, and Evelyn. We learned that Evelyn's drive to uncover her roots was fueled by a deep, unrecognized connection to her ancestors.

In the end, we fulfilled Lillian's final request. We found her great-granddaughter and she knows the truth. This revelation brought closure to a story that had been buried for far too long.

As we leave Maplewood Mansion, we do so with a sense of accomplishment and a renewed commitment to uncovering the hidden truths that linger in the shadows of history.

But our journey doesn't end here. Join us next time as we explore the haunted Hawthorne Hall, where the ghosts of vaudeville performers from a bygone era continue to captivate and terrify those who dare to enter. Until then, remember: sometimes, the past refuses to stay buried."

CHAPTER 18

"Great job everyone," Roger Pinnacle swiveled around in his desk chair and made a temple with his fingers in front of his face.

"Yes, you have a powerful story here," someone whose name I'd already forgotten said.

"Thank you." I said. I looked at the others also sitting around the table, appearing to be just as confused as I was feeling.

"We're glad you like it. We only wish we could do more."

"What do you mean? Of course you're doing more. You signed a contract, right?" Mr. Pinnacle looked at his assistant. "They signed a contract, right? Find the contracts. Make sure they signed them."

His assistant nodded brusquely and ran from the room.

"Oh, no need," I tried to stop him. "We did sign contracts, but Mia Sanchez told us we were fired. That the network wasn't picking up the show."

Several of the well-appointed people in the room muttered to themselves and to each other. Mr. Pinnacle held up a hand.

"Ms. Sanchez is no longer with the company. We were skeptical when she kept reporting these bonkers things happening on your set. But then when she told an outrageous story about finding you running down a street carrying a, what was it?" He looked at the man on his left.

"A skull," he said.

"Yes! A skull! Imagine that. We started looking into her a bit more and discovered she was skimming from the company. She only made it worse when she accused you of leaving the skull in her car and cursing her! Said that was the only reason she got caught!"

Mr. Pinnacle and the others enjoyed a good round of belly laughs I tried to share.

Ollie kicked me under the table and made a show of smiling at me with her eyes wide.

I got the message and laughed with them. "Yes, can you imagine?" I said.

"Anyway, she is no longer with the company and we are looking for your new producer now. In the meantime, I believe you have a few weeks off and then you're off to...where? Somebody tell me where they are going next!" He bellowed.

By now, his assistant had returned with the signed contracts and laid them on the table. "Hawthorne Hall," he whispered.

"Hawthorne Hall! Just as I thought! So good luck to you all. I can't wait to see the next installment."

He swiveled his chair back around and we were dismissed.

We filed out of the office and stood in the waiting area.

"So, I guess we do have jobs after all," Ollie said.

"Tyler, I didn't know you recorded the ending part. When did you do that?" I asked.

"Right after they told me we weren't fired. Which, by the way, was yesterday. I knew they were bringing the rest of you in and wanted to let it be a surprise."

"Is everyone still on board?" I asked, looking around at the team.

Despite their plans to move onto other projects, they all were adamant that they were available and absolutely weren't going anywhere.

"So, where are we going next?" Leo asked, a grin spreading across his face.

"Hawthorne Hall," Tyler said. "Here, they gave me this just before the meeting."

He passed a manila folder to me.

I opened it and pulled out the documents inside. The top sheet was an old, sepia-toned photograph of a grand theater, its marquee boasting the names of long-forgotten vaudeville acts. Below the photo was a modern-day picture of the same theater, now dilapidated and abandoned.

"Hawthorne Hall," I read aloud, "was a famous vaudeville venue in its heyday, but it's been closed for decades. Recently, there have been reports of strange occurrences—ghostly apparitions, eerie music, and unexplained noises. It seems to be haunted by the spirits of performers from the past."

Ollie leaned over to look at the pictures. "A haunted theater? That sounds incredible."

I continued reading. "Witnesses have reported seeing ghostly figures in old vaudeville costumes, hearing laughter and applause from an empty theater, and even seeing performances on the stage when the building is supposed to be empty. There are rumors that some acts who performed there might have met tragic ends."

"Any connections to the present day? I'm

wondering if there may be a reason these hauntings are still going on," Ethan said.

"Yes," I said. "It says here that there are a few descendants of the original performers who still live in the area. They've reported feeling a strange pull towards the theater, as if something is calling them back."

"Excellent," Ethan said with a grin.

"This sounds like an incredible story, Jackie," Ollie said. "I can't wait."

I nodded, feeling a surge of anticipation. "Agreed. Hawthorne Hall is going to be a fascinating assignment. We'll uncover the history, connect with the present, and find out what's really haunting that place."

As the team discussed plans and logistics, I couldn't help but feel a thrill of excitement. The journey to Maplewood Mansion had been intense and emotional, but it had also bonded us as a team and prepared us for whatever would come next.

As we walked to the elevator, Emily's eyes sparkled. "Imagine the stories we will uncover. The history of vaudeville is fascinating, and those performers led such interesting lives. They were like us. I mean, like a family, you know?"

As the elevator doors closed, Gabby flapped her wings and began whistling the theme to the Addams Family.

Ned: *I told my wife, Nellie, she should learn to embrace her mistakes.*
Nellie: *I agreed, so I gave him a hug.*

Meet Ned and Nellie, the Vaudevillian stars of Haunting at Hawthorne Hall, book 2 in the Haunted Histories series. Grab your copy now!

They will keep you laughing all the way to your grave....

I'd love to stay in touch! If you would like to receive free monthly updates, sneak peeks, and specials, join my Patreon!

If you enjoyed this book, please consider leaving a review or star rating. It's one of the best ways to support independent authors and it lets others know if they might also enjoy this book.

Scan the QR code above to see other books by

Lynn M. Stout.

Scan the QR code above to join my free Patreon and
receive updates and special deals monthly.